SAM

a novel

SAM

a novel

Luke F Harris

GWENDOLINE PRESS

ISBN 978-0-473-37184-5

Wellington, New Zealand

Copyright © Luke F Harris 2016

GWENDOLINE PRESS

For Mum and Dad

Contents

chapter one

"GET OUT OF bed this instant!"

Tom rolled onto his side and pulled the pillow over his head with a groan. The shrillness of his sister's voice seemed to pierce his skull.

For the past hour, he had been staring at the bedroom ceiling. In the far corner, a tiny black spider was industriously repairing its web. He watched, mesmerised, as it plucked at the silk thread, oblivious to the world below. God, how he envied the spider.

It must be nine by now, he thought, glancing at the blank screen of his alarm clock. It was becoming a habit, lying in bed all morning.

The alarm clock had packed up weeks ago but was still sitting on the bedside table, gathering dust. He reached across the bed and pulled back the curtain a couple of centimetres. The sun had already cleared the ridge of hills opposite and was now inching its way across a cloudless blue sky.

It hadn't rained anywhere in the North Island for weeks, and by the looks of it, today wasn't going to be any different. The six o'clock news the previous evening had led with the story of a Waikato farmer whose business was on the brink of collapse.

"How do you feel?" the grinning news anchor had asked, the camera panning across what had once been a lush green paddock but now looked more like barren wasteland.

"Fucking marvellous," he had replied on the farmer's behalf and had changed the channel without watching any more.

He gazed out the window. The trees at the bottom of the garden were in full bloom. He watched as a tui flitted happily from tree to tree, the white tuft on its throat gleaming in the morning sunshine.

He let go of the curtain, flopped back onto the mattress and closed his eyes. Whoever had said that hell was other people had been right on the money.

"I take it you haven't eaten yet?" His sister appeared in the doorway. She looked like their mother, standing there with her hands on her hips. He shook his head.

Five minutes later he was sitting at the kitchen table, a mug of steaming hot tea and a plate of toast in front of him.

"I put the Vegemite on extra thick—the way you like."

"Thanks," he said. He didn't realise just how hungry he was until he took the first bite. "Look," he mumbled through a mouthful of toast. He swallowed what he was chewing and washed it down with a slurp of tea. "I've got work to do."

"Don't make me laugh," Carla replied.

He glowered at her over his toast as he took another bite. "I'm fine. You don't need to keep checking up on me. I'm not going to do anything stupid." He didn't tell her that he had considered 'doing something stupid' several times.

He stood and carried his breakfast back to the living room. Carla followed him.

"I'm glad to hear it," she said, sitting down next to him on the sofa and tucking her bare feet up underneath her. "When was the last time you left this house?" she asked. His sister had never been one to beat around the bush.

He shrugged his shoulders.

"I know you don't like talking about things," she continued, unfazed by his silence. "You've always been the same."

He felt his stomach muscles contract. He and his sister had always been close. He knew better than to try to lie to her. Like the proverbial dog with a bone, she wouldn't give up until he had told her what she wanted to know.

"It's OK," she blew on her tea and then took a small sip, "to talk about stuff."

He reached for the remote, which was balanced on the arm of the sofa, and turned on the television instead. His sister sighed.

"You can't go on like this. It's been three months now."

He munched on his toast and flicked through the channels as if he hadn't heard her. He paused on the weather channel and feigned interest in the forecast.

"I bet you haven't left this house more than half a dozen times. When was the last time you had a shower?" She leaned in and sniffed his T-shirt.

"Get out of it," he growled, and as he shoved her away, a wave of tea sloshed over the side of her mug, into her lap. She jumped to her feet and ran to the kitchen for a cloth.

"Sorry," he said when she reappeared. She was dabbing at her pants with a tea towel. She looked up and glared.

"How's Olivia?" he asked, quickly changing the subject. Carla rolled her eyes and continued to blot at her jeans. "What's she done this time?" He wasn't sure he wanted to know the answer.

He got up off the sofa and followed her back into the kitchen.

"What hasn't she done, you mean?" Carla replied. She sat down at the kitchen table and started to flick through one of the unopened newspapers. He made a mental note to cancel his subscription. A dozen pages in, she stopped and leaned back in her chair. "She's met a boy." She pushed the paper away. "Need I say more?"

"You met Adam when you were sixteen."

"And look how that turned out," she laughed caustically.

He sat down opposite her. The steam from his tea fogged up his glasses. "Remember when you brought Adam home the first time? I thought Dad was going to kill him and bury his body in the back yard."

Carla smiled, but her eyes looked sad.

He would never forget that afternoon, twenty years before, when his sister had introduced Adam to their father. She should have known that arriving on the back of a Harley was only going to provoke a reaction. *Or perhaps she had known that all along,* he thought.

"Speaking of Olivia," Carla said. He had a fair idea

of what was coming next but he stayed silent. "I was thinking that you could maybe have a word to her. She's only got a year of college to go, and if she doesn't pull her finger out soon, she can kiss goodbye to varsity."

He took a deep breath. "You think she'll listen to me?" And for the first time in months, he almost laughed. The idea of him counselling anybody, let alone a sixteen-year-old girl, was ridiculous.

"Well, she won't listen to me. I swear she does the exact opposite of anything I tell her just to spite me."

He stood up and walked over to the pantry. It was cram packed with food, none of which he had purchased. His friends and family clearly had low opinions of his ability to survive. The fact that he had lived by himself before he met Sam counted for nothing.

"I know there's a packet of biscuits in here somewhere," he said, searching each shelf. He found the biscuits hiding behind a family-size pack of Weet-Bix at the back of the cupboard. He tore open the foil wrapper and offered the packet to Carla. "Can't Adam talk to her?" he asked, dunking a biscuit in his mug of tea. "He *is* her father, after all."

Carla seemed to deflate at the mention of her ex-husband. "Who knows where he is? I haven't heard a peep out of him in weeks. Last weekend, he was supposed to take the kids to the movies, but he didn't show up."

She looked as if she were carrying the weight of the world on her shoulders, and he felt his resolve beginning to weaken.

"Look, I'm sure she'll be fine," he said, getting to his

feet before he agreed to anything that he would later regret. He tipped the remainder of his tea down the sink and put the biscuits back in the pantry. "She's a smart girl—far smarter than we ever were."

"So you won't talk to her, then?" Carla crossed her arms over her chest.

He should have known not to hesitate.

Carla snatched her handbag off the bench and marched out the kitchen. She was halfway to the front door before he caught up with her.

"Carla." He made a grab for her arm, but she yanked it away.

"I'm sorry about what happened to Sam," she said, "I really am, Tom. But you're not the only one who has problems."

He waited until she had driven off before he closed the door and went back to bed.

HE SPENT MOST of the afternoon and evening in the garage, tinkering with his bike. It was months since he had last ridden it, and its warrant of fitness was already long overdue. He was so absorbed in what he was doing that it was almost dark before he realised the light was fading. He put down the wrench he was holding, clambered to his feet, and retreated into the house, his arms full of oily engine parts.

He spread an old newspaper over the kitchen table and carefully arranged the various parts into neat rows, wiping his hands on his pants when he had finished. In the morning, he would reassemble the engine and ride the bike down to the local garage to be signed off.

I'll just close my eyes for a moment, he thought, dropping exhausted onto the sofa and propping his feet on the coffee table. The sun had now disappeared behind the western hills, out of sight, and the last rays of the day illuminated the thin, wispy clouds from below, so that they shone like pure gold.

The first rap on the front door failed to wake him fully. He nuzzled his face into the soft fabric of the couch and scratched the side of his nose. *Sam will get that*, he thought, his mind drifting between sleep and consciousness. The second knock was distinctly louder and brought him to his senses with a jolt.

He sat up and rubbed his eyes. He squinted at his watch and slowly the hands came into focus. It was half past nine; he had been asleep for over an hour.

With a sigh, he got to his feet, stretched, and wandered over to the French doors.

A thick blanket of sea fog had glided in off the Cook Strait, concealing the airport below. The tail of a Boeing 737 sliced through the cloud like a shark's fin and disappeared again into the mist.

He hadn't taken two steps before there was a third knock, followed by raised voices. "I'm coming!" he shouted.

"She yours?" asked the police officer standing on the doorstep. For a moment, he was struck dumb. Flanked on either side by uniformed officers stood his niece. She had her arms crossed and a look of defiance on her face.

"Not quite," he replied, finding his voice at last. He glared at Olivia. "She belongs to my sister."

"Well, she told us she lived here," the other officer

continued. "We found her spray-painting a fence. Luckily for her, the owner doesn't want to press charges. If she cleans it off, he'll let the matter drop." The officer gave Olivia a contemptuous look. "Bloody youths."

"Get inside," he said to his niece. Without looking up, she uncrossed her arms and pushed past him into the house. Thankfully, the officers seemed as eager as he was to end the conversation and barked, "Just make sure she cleans it off, otherwise we may be forced to take the matter further."

He nodded politely and closed the door.

"What the hell?" he cursed. He forced himself to take a deep breath.

Olivia was slouched on the sofa flicking through the channels on the TV when Tom walked into the living room. He went straight over to the television and turned it off at the wall. "Hey, I was watching that," Olivia protested, but he paid no notice.

"What the hell just happened?" he said.

She didn't answer. She stared straight ahead at the blank screen. "Fuck!" he cursed in frustration.

He was standing at the kitchen sink peeling potatoes when Olivia finally appeared in the doorway. Without saying a word, she walked over to the kitchen table and sat down. He kept his eyes on the growing mound of peelings in the sink.

"So your exams are coming up soon?" The atmosphere was almost unbearable. If he didn't say something now, they would probably sit in silence for ever. "Are you ready?"

Olivia didn't reply immediately. "I guess so," she

mumbled. Her eyes scanned the engine parts laid out across the table.

"What do you want to do when you finish school?" he persevered.

It was now pitch-black outside. He looked through his reflection in the window, towards the flickering trail of red and yellow lights on the other side of the harbour. *Where are you when I need you, Sam?*

He plunged his hand into the ice-cold water and plucked out another potato.

"I'm talking to you," he raised his voice. "What are you going to do when you leave school?"

Olivia looked up at him and shrugged her shoulders. "I don't know. Mum wants me to go to university. She says that if I don't get qualifications I'll end up old and miserable like her." She started to chip away at the black nail polish on her right hand.

He could feel himself getting irritated. "And you don't think she's got a point?"

"Well, you didn't go to university."

"My life's hardly been a fucking success story," he snapped and instantly regretted it. "I'm sorry," he apologised, "I shouldn't have lost my temper."

"Doesn't matter. I've heard worse."

After tea they watched television for an hour before he drove Olivia home.

The wind was picking up again from the south and the orange air sock at the end of the runway was flying almost horizontal. As they drove along Calabar Road, he felt the wind tug at the steering wheel. The radio was switched off and the silence was broken only momentarily by the roar of a twin-engine jet coming in to land. Olivia still hadn't spoken by the time they pulled up outside Carla's house.

"Don't give your mum a hard time when you go inside, please." He didn't cut the engine; instead, he waited, one foot on the clutch and the other on the brake. As soon as she disappeared into the house, he swung the car round and sped off back towards the eastern suburbs.

He didn't take the direct route home. Instead, he drove up through Newtown to Island Bay and took the coastal road round the southern tip of the island. He hadn't ventured so far from home in months—in fact, he could count on one hand the number of times he had left the peninsula—but now, having been forced to drive halfway across the city, he didn't feel in any particular rush to get home.

A quarter of an hour later, he was turning the corner into Breaker Bay. He pulled over onto the gravel at the side of the road and turned off the headlights.

The lights from the houses along the bay were reflected in water close to the shore, but further out the ocean was black. He wound down the window and took a deep breath, his lungs burning as they inflated with ice-cold Antarctic air. He pulled up the collar of his coat, removed the keys from the ignition, and climbed out of the car.

The gravel crunched underfoot as he made his way down to the water's edge. As he vaulted over the wooden barrier that separated the car park from the beach, he felt the first drops of rain fall.

He perched on a rock, the water lapping below, and watched as the evening ferry from Picton glided northward, towards the safety of the harbour. The ship, a mass of sparkling lights, looked remarkably peaceful, but he knew better. The last time that he and Sam had made the three-hour crossing, he had been violently seasick. Afterwards, he had vowed never to step foot on a boat again.

Within minutes, the rain drops had trebled in size. *It won't be long until the storm makes landfall*, he thought, and felt a trickle of freezing cold water run down the back of his neck. He hunched his shoulders and thrust his hands into the pockets of his duck-down jacket. *Perhaps if I sit here for long enough, the southerly will numb my brain as well*, he wondered. He was tired of thinking—tired of feeling sad.

It was then that his fingers registered a small cylindrical object at the bottom of his pocket. He removed the container and held it up close to his face so that he could read the small print in the dark—Diazepam. "Hello, my little friends," he said. He had forgotten completely about that particular stash.

Those first few weeks after the funeral were still a blur. They probably always would be. At one point—looking back, he wasn't sure quite how she had managed it— Carla had convinced him to see a doctor.

The doctor had taken one look at his sunken, bloodshot eyes and had prescribed a cocktail of pills. "I'm not depressed," he vaguely remembered protesting, "but I'll take the ones to make me sleep."

He held the plastic container between his thumb and index finger and stared at the little white tablets inside. Without giving it much thought, he unscrewed the cap and upended the bottle into the palm of his hand.

It would be so easy. So easy. The thought that it could all be over before the night was out was enticing. No more grief. No more thinking. Nothing.

"Life's one big head fuck," he had told Carla only the other day. "We're born—we don't ask to be born, by the way—we work our arses off for thirty or forty years, and then, just when we think we've got it made, life comes along and screws us in the arse."

"You've got such a poetic way with words." She had laughed and then given him a bear hug.

He looked down at the palm of his hand. He had never taken the easy way out before, and deep down he knew that he never would.

Quickly, before he changed his mind, he jumped up, walked down to the water's edge and threw open his hand. For a nanosecond the tiny tablets flashed white in the darkness, and then they were gone.

chapter two

TOM EYEBALLED THE computer screen. His eyes were beginning to ache, and he could feel the muscles in the back of his neck getting tighter. He gripped the mouse in his left hand and dragged the cursor across the page. *No going back now*, he told himself, and double-clicked.

The sky was already darkening in the east, and the lights of the houses on the surrounding hills flickered on one by one. The solitary wind turbine that towered over the suburb of Brooklyn would soon vanish for another night.

As he stood up, he caught a glimpse of his own reflection in the window and paused. Hesitantly, he raised a hand his face, to the lines on his forehead, the creases around his eyes. God, when had he got so old? He seemed to have aged ten years over the past twelve months.

With a sigh, he slipped the laptop into its case and returned it to the antique bureau in the hall. The desk-cum-sideboard was a rimu monstrosity that he had been guilted into taking after his grandfather died. When he got back from his trip, he would sell it, and to hell with the consequences.

Speaking of family, he hadn't seen Carla for a couple of days. Although he had enjoyed the peace and quiet to begin with, he was starting to crave human contact. Even the cat had been keeping his distance.

Cats don't really bring a lot to the party, now, do they? he could hear his grandfather saying. He smiled at the memory. Yet again, he had been right on the money. In exchange for food and shelter, his own cat was systematically destroying the house.

He wandered over to the kitchen bench, lifted the phone from its cradle, and pressed the speed-dial button number one.

He let the phone ring for longer than he normally would have. Nobody in his sister's house ever paid attention to the phone, and he knew the odds were that at least one person was home. After what felt like an eternity, there was a click on the other end of the line.

"Yeah," a voice grunted into the receiver.

"Just the person I wanted to talk to." He tried to sound as cheerful as possible, but his enthusiasm met with a stony silence. "I really need your help with something important tomorrow morning."

"Yeah."

"Can you be ready to go at seven?"

"Are you crazy?" Olivia asked, her voice suddenly becoming animated. "It's the school holidays."

"Make it eight then, but no later. We'll have a drive ahead of us, and I don't want to get stuck in traffic."

"Where are we going?" she asked. Now she sounded intrigued. He didn't have the heart to tell her not to get too excited.

"I'll tell you tomorrow. I'll have you back by early afternoon. Is your mum there?" he asked, changing the subject.

"Uh-huh." He heard a clunk as she dropped the receiver on the sideboard and yelled for Carla at the top of her lungs.

He turned and looked at the photo of Sam grinning back at him from the windowsill. "You'd better bloody appreciate this," he said aloud and smiled.

There was another long pause before he heard the sound of jandals slip-slapping against the wooden floorboards. The footsteps got louder and louder as his sister approached the phone and then stopped altogether. "Tom, is that you?"

"Uh-huh."

"Is everything OK?"

He could hear that she wasn't in a good mood. "Yeah, everything is fine. Look, what you said about talking to Olivia—I'll do it."

Although he couldn't see her face, he heard her sigh with relief. "Thanks, Tom. I appreciate it. Just tell her that she needs to take the next few years seriously—"

"Uh-huh."

"And make her understand that boys can wait. I don't want her making the same mistakes I did and get tied down to some waster—"

"Look," he cut her off, "do you want to talk to her instead?"

"OK, OK. It's just that I'm worried."

"I know you are, but I really don't think you need to be. She's got her head screwed on right. I'll be there at eight on the dot. Just make sure she's ready."

"Thanks, Tom," Carla said. She sounded a lot more cheerful than she had only a minute before. "Love you."

"Yeah, you too," he replied, and hung up the phone.

THE NEXT MORNING he pulled up outside his sister's house at a quarter to eight and blasted the horn three times. The curtains were still drawn but he was reluctant to leave the warmth of the car to knock on the door.

It was a fresh morning, and there wasn't a wisp of cloud in the blue expanse of sky. "The gods must be smiling on you," he said, looking in the rear-view mirror at the wooden box on the back seat.

Ten minutes passed before the front door opened and Olivia emerged. She had a cellphone in one hand and a can of Coke in the other.

"Where are we going?" she asked, dropping onto the front passenger seat and pulling the door shut with a thud. Her eyes stayed glued to the cellphone while she spoke.

"Castlepoint," he replied. He put the car into gear and pulled out into the traffic with a wheel spin.

Olivia put her phone in her lap and looked at him. She had a confused expression on her face.

"We're going to scatter Sam's ashes," he explained. "Sam wanted you to be there, so I'm taking you."

"And you don't want me to be?"

"Don't be silly," he replied. In fact, he didn't want to be there either.

Fifty minutes later they were clear of the city and winding their way up the Rimutakas. The previous

24

winter the road had been closed for two days because of heavy snowfall, and the commuters from Masterton and the other towns dotted along State Highway 2 had been forced to abandon their cars and crowd onto the Wellington-bound train instead. But that was more than six months ago, and there was no trace of the grey sludge that had covered the grass verges for weeks.

Olivia didn't like heights and she kept her eyes down as they wound their way up the mountain. The road came close to the edge in several places, the sheer drop down to the thick bush below unnervingly close.

After a windy ten-minute ascent, they passed the summit and dropped down onto the grassy plains of the Wairarapa. The weather was always better over the hill, and today was no exception.

"What are we stopping for?" Olivia asked when he stopped on the high street in Featherston.

"I'm hungry. You want anything?" He nodded at a bakery across the street. Olivia shook her head. "Suit yourself then."

As he waited patiently for his trim flat white—extra shot, no sugar—he scanned the rogues gallery on the wall behind the counter. "How long ago was that taken?" he asked, pointing at a signed photograph of a well-known All Black.

"Since a long time before," the lady making his coffee answered in what sounded like a Dutch accent, but she didn't offer any more information.

She heaped two large sugars into a polystyrene cup, filled it with coffee and lukewarm milk, and passed it across the counter. "Four dollars, please."

He paid with a five-dollar note and dropped the change into the charity tin next to the till. He didn't hurry back to the car but sat down at one of the café's weather-beaten patio tables.

He took a sip of his coffee and promptly spat it onto the pavement. It was truly awful.

Olivia was still sitting in the car, her feet propped on the dashboard. He could see she was talking to someone on her cellphone, and from the grin on her face, he knew it wasn't his sister. *Carla's going to have her work cut out there*, he thought, standing up and tossing the full cup into the nearest bin.

"You OK?" Oliva asked, as he slipped the seatbelt over his shoulder.

"Yep," he answered and started the engine.

They drove in silence for the next ten minutes. Olivia gazed listlessly out the window as the countryside whizzed by in a green blur.

"You're addicted to that thing," he said when she had checked her phone for the third time in as many minutes. "Who were you talking to before?"

"Nobody."

"Nobody, eh?"

"Nobody you'd know."

He waited another minute before trying again. "So what's his name?"

"Who?"

"Come on, don't play dumb. I wasn't born yesterday. The boy you were speaking to before. I saw the way you were smiling back there. Is it serious?"

Olivia seemed to squirm in her seat. "You can't tell Mum."

"I think she already knows."

"Fuck."

"Language, please," he felt duty bound to say. He didn't really care whether she swore, but he knew Carla wouldn't approve.

"His name's George. He's in his first year of uni."

"Older guy, eh?" he winked, and nudged her in the ribs to try to lighten the mood.

"If you're going to take the piss, I won't tell you," she snapped. She crossed her arms and turned to face the window again.

"OK, I'm sorry. It's serious though?"

"I dunno," she replied. "We've only been seeing each other for a month. We haven't even done it yet."

"Whoa!" This time it was his turn to squirm, and he let the subject drop immediately. There was a long pause before either of them was ready to speak again.

"Do you think you'll meet someone else?"

Olivia's question came from left-field and caught him completely off-guard. He opened his mouth to speak, but then closed it again without saying a word.

"I don't know," he answered at last, casting a guilty look in the rear-view mirror at the casket sitting on the back seat. "No, I don't think so."

By the time they reached Castlepoint, the weather had begun to close in. Strong gusts of wind buffeted the car as they crawled the last fifty metres along the gravel track that led to the beach.

He pulled the car into the makeshift car park and cut the engine.

Up on the rocks sat the lighthouse, majestic, towering

over the beach. It looked exactly the same as it had the last time he had been here—with Sam. Nothing had changed.

And yet everything had changed.

"You ready?" he sighed, waking from his daydream and turning to look at Olivia, who was tapping away on her phone, a look of extreme concentration on her face.

She grunted in reply, slid the phone into her pocket, and opened the door. But she wasn't holding on to the handle tightly enough. A gust of wind caught the door, yanked it wide open, and the litter in the passenger foot well flew across the sand.

He put on his windbreaker and rubbed his hands together to get the blood flowing through his fingers. "Bloody cold, eh?" He pulled the hood of his jacket over his head and tightened the drawstrings.

"You look silly," Olivia laughed. She walked around the car and loosened the hood for him. "That's better," she said. "We're not going skiing, you know?"

Slowly, they wound their way up the footpath that led to the lighthouse; Olivia out in front, him trailing behind, the wooden box clutched to his chest. By the time they reached the top, he was wheezing and beads of sweat were running down his forehead, into his eyes. *When did I get so unfit?* he thought, placing the box gently on the ground and leaning back against the handrail until he got his breath back.

At the top of the slope, they skirted around the lighthouse, past a solitary Japanese tourist gazing intently at a plaque on the wall, and climbed over the wooden fence, out onto the rocks.

28

The wind was even stronger beyond the shelter of the lighthouse, and for a moment, he thought they might have to abandon the idea altogether and retreat to the car. Yet when he looked up to tell Olivia to be careful, she was already a good ten metres ahead, leaning into the wind, her long blonde hair blowing wildly behind her.

"Wait up!" he yelled, holding the wooden box as tight as he could. He scanned the rocks for cracks, for fear of tripping and dropping the casket. "If you fall into the ocean, your mum will kill me." But Olivia was too far in front to hear him.

For the past three months, Sam's ashes had sat on the dresser in his bedroom. Ashes collecting dust. *How ironic*, he thought, and clutched the box even tighter.

He knew that Sam wouldn't want to be kept on display, like an old relic—they had talked about it briefly, before he had changed the subject—yet even now he wasn't sure he would actually be able to let go. A box of grit was all he had left. Grit that would be gone in a few moments' time.

"Shouldn't we say something?" Olivia asked. Her eyes welled with tears.

He stared straight out to sea, at the endless expanse of blue that stretched out to the horizon and beyond.

"Somewhere out there is South America," he said, speaking to himself, to Olivia, to the casket in his arms. "We never made it to South America."

He sensed Olivia moving closer.

"We were planning to go when—" His words trailed off on the wind. He turned and looked at Olivia, whose tears had already been blown dry.

"Ready?" she asked.

He took a deep breath. "Ready."

Gently, he lifted the lid and unscrewed the cap on the square plastic container inside. "Hold this," he said, passing the cap to Olivia.

The wind, still howling from the southeast, was driving the large white-capped waves onto the jagged rocks below, sending plumes of water several metres into the air. Slowly, he extended his arms until the casket was perpendicular to his body.

"I'm not sure that I can," he said, suddenly overwhelmed by the finality of what they were doing. He hadn't thought it would be this difficult.

Olivia reached out and placed a hand on his. She rested her head on his shoulder. "We'll do it together."

"Sam would be really proud of you today," he replied, turning and kissing his niece on the top of her head.

"Right, Sammy, it's off to South America for you!" he said. And with one, resolute movement, before he could change his mind, they turned the urn upside down.

Neither of them had been paying any attention to the direction of the wind, which had changed to the south and increased in intensity. At the exact same instant the ashes came pouring out of the box, a strong gust whipped up from below and sent them flying back in their faces.

Blinded, his eyes, nose and mouth full of ash, he dropped the empty box. He heard it go tumbling over the edge and shatter on the rocks below.

"Are—you—OK?" he struggled to speak between

coughing fits. It was a full minute before he was able to breathe properly again.

With red, watery eyes, his hair full of grit, he stumbled back towards the fence and the safety of the lighthouse. Olivia had already taken off her coat and was beating it against the wall.

They walked all the way back to the car in silence.

"Fuck!" he cursed, thumping the steering wheel, once they were back in the warm. Olivia turned to him, an earnest look on her face."

"I don't think Sam wanted to do South America," she said.

He looked back at her in disbelief. Then, for the first time in he didn't know how long, he actually laughed—a muscle-wrenching laugh that brought on another coughing fit. "Let's get going," he wheezed. "At least you'll never forget today, eh."

"I think I'm traumatised, Uncle Tom, but a beer ought to fix that."

"Nice try," he laughed again, and swung the car around, towards home.

chapter three

SAM HAD BEEN revising for his college finals since before breakfast, and the clock on the wall was now fast approaching five o'clock. He stretched his arms, yawned, and leaned back in his chair.

His bedroom was a complete mess. Textbooks and scraps of paper littered every surface including the bed. In the corner, Patch was curled up, fast asleep. The light streaming in through the open window gave his black coat a copper glow.

Sam took a deep breath and picked up his pen. Quickly, before he changed his mind again, he jotted down the answer he had been mulling over for the past twenty minutes. He flicked to the answer section at the back of the textbook.

"Come on!" he cursed and threw his pen across the room in frustration. He put his face in his hands and let out a low groan. Patch looked up and cocked his head to one side.

The coffee his mother had made him was still sitting on his desk, untouched. He picked it up and took a sip. It was stone cold. He spat it straight back into the mug and wiped a hand across his mouth.

"I guess it's time we took you for a walk," he sighed. Patch was on his feet and out the door before Sam had finished speaking.

All the way to the beach, Patch pulled on his lead. Each time a cyclist or a bus whizzed past, he lunged forward and almost garrotted himself.

"Heel!" Sam scolded again and yanked hard on the lead. Reluctantly, Patch fell in beside him. But as soon as they reached Lyall Bay, he was off like a shot, careening down the beach towards the water, scattering the seagulls that were clustered together on the sand. The gulls squawked angrily as they took to the air.

Sam perched on a rock at the far end of the bay and watched as Patch sniffed a piece of driftwood that had washed up on the shore overnight.

For the past month, Sam had barely seen the light of day, and now, with less than twenty-four hours until his final exam, he felt as if his head was about to implode. He rubbed at his eyes and yawned so wide that his jaw gave a disturbing crack.

Never before in his life had he been so nervous. If he didn't pass tomorrow's exam, chances were he wouldn't get Bursary—and if he didn't get Bursary, he could kiss goodbye to his place at the University of Otago.

Half a dozen surfers were bobbing about on the water, waiting patiently for the perfect wave. As he was watching, one of the surfers jumped to his feet, glided several metres across the water, and face-planted into the swell. Patch was busy darting in and out of the waves, snapping at the foam as it lapped around his legs.

The peacefulness of the moment was shattered in the next instant, when a beat-up, old ute came roaring down the road, its windows down and its stereo blaring. It slowed as it reached the gravel car park at the east end of the beach and bumped up the kerb. Two young guys hopped down from the cab.

The one who'd been driving had short brown hair, and as he reached into the tailboard of the ute to untie his surfboard, his T-shirt rode up his back to reveal a strip of tanned skin. He pulled two wetsuits out of the truck, handed one to his friend, and disappeared behind the vehicle to change. Clearly, his friend wasn't nearly as self-conscious. He unbuttoned his shorts and let them drop to the ground right where he stood, revealing his snow-white buttocks to the world.

Sam gulped and turned away before anybody caught him looking.

"Hey, mister," a voice called to him from the beach below. He almost jumped out of his skin. He looked down to find a freckly kid of about five or six gawping up at him. The boy smiled, revealing two missing front teeth. "Is that your dog?" He pointed down the beach.

Patch was bounding towards them, a long piece of driftwood clenched between his teeth. The log protruded at least a metre on either side of his jaw, and as Patch snaked his way across the sand, the branch seesawed precariously from side to side. He winced as Patch narrowly missed a young couple with a small child.

"Patch!" he yelled at the top of his lungs, tossing his cigarette between two rocks and jumping down onto the sand. He started down the beach towards Patch, who was quickly gaining on a jogger pacing along the water's edge.

"Patch, stop!" he shouted. But he was too late. As Patch flew past, the wooden branch clipped the jogger on the back of the legs, just behind his left knee. He seemed to go down in slow motion, like a soldier who had taken a bullet to the chest.

"I'm so, so sorry," he apologised, stopping just shy of the jogger, who was lying face down in the sand. "Are you all right?"

Patch had dropped the piece of driftwood immediately and was now sniffing at the rotting carcass of a fish.

"Are you OK?" he asked again. He wasn't sure he wanted to know the answer.

"Yeah," the guy said, waving away his hand. He pushed himself to his feet and brushed the sand from his arms and legs. "No thanks to your dog, though." His shorts and T-shirt were soaking wet, but, thankfully, he appeared to be uninjured.

Sam let go the breath he had been holding and asked, "Are you sure?"

Not only was the guy much younger than he had first thought—he couldn't be any older than twenty-four or twenty-five—he was also gorgeous. He had thick, shoulder-length blond hair and the bluest eyes Sam had ever seen.

"Yeah, I'll live," the guy said, replacing his earphones, which had been knocked out of his ears in the fall, and jogged on up the beach.

Sam looked for Patch and spotted him sniffing around the dunes by the surf club, his tail poking up above the long grass like the periscope on a submarine. *At least he's not annoying anybody,* he told himself, and walked up to the road and sat on the stone wall. The southerly wind was bitter, but he was loath to return to his revision just yet.

He took the cigarettes out of his pocket and tapped one from the packet. He lit the end, cupped a hand in front of his mouth, and inhaled deeply. As his lungs filled with warm, dry smoke, his heartbeat began to return to normal.

The rhythmic crashing of the waves against the shore was almost hypnotic, and he let his thoughts drift away on the wind. It didn't seem possible that in just a few months' time, everything he had ever known would be hundreds of kilometres away. University, Dunedin, leaving home—suddenly, it all felt real, and he wasn't sure that he was ready. Not just yet.

While he was still daydreaming, the blond-haired jogger reached the end of the beach, turned, and started back the way he had just come. He came to a stop almost directly in front of where Sam was sitting. His T-shirt clung to the muscles on his back as he leaned forward to stretch his hamstrings. He didn't have the typical runner's physique—thin and sinewy—he looked more like a rugby player. His shoulders and thighs were solid muscle.

He could see Patch out of the corner of his eye. He had managed to ingratiate himself with a group of teenagers and was devouring hot chips by the handful. He put his fingers in his mouth and whistled. Patch's ears pricked up at once. He whistled again, and Patch came skulking back, his tail tucked between his legs.

"Come on, you," he said, grabbing him by the collar and slipping the lead over his head. "I think you've caused enough trouble for one day. If we don't get home soon, Mum'll flip her lid."

His FATHER WOULD come home steaming drunk at least twice a week. He would pour himself a scotch, light a cigarette, and fall asleep in front of the television. The chocolate-brown armchair in the living room was covered with burn marks. The fact that they hadn't all burned alive in their beds was a miracle in itself.

At half past ten, he finally called time on his revision. What he didn't know now, he figured he never would. Even if he had wanted to continue, he didn't think he would be able to keep his eyes open much longer. He pulled off his clothes, dropped them on the floor where he stood, and crawled into bed. His arms and legs felt as heavy as lead, and as he rolled over onto his front, he imagined his body sinking through the mattress.

He was fast asleep when the front door swung open and slammed against the wall. The impact reverberated through the entire house. *Earthquake*, he thought, still half dreaming. He rubbed at his eyes and rolled onto his side, ready to get out of bed at the next shake. Instead, he heard his father's voice. Slowly, the pieces of the jigsaw fell into place.

The bedroom door creaked open as Patch sloped back into the room and curled up beside the bed. He let his arm hang over the edge of the mattress and felt the wetness of Patch's nose brush against the back of his hand. Patch gave his fingers an affectionate lick. "Go to sleep," he murmured. As he retracted his hand, he wiped it on the fitted sheet.

An hour later, he was still wide awake.

With a sigh, he reached for the cord of his bedside lamp and ran his fingers along the wire until he found the switch. It took a minute for his eyes to adjust to the glare of the light. The hands on his wind-up alarm clock pointed to half past midnight.

Next to the clock, serving as coaster to a glass of water, was a dog-eared prospectus for the University of Otago. He moved the glass aside and picked up the booklet. On the cover was a large embossed photo of two students, strolling arm in arm across the campus. *They look far too happy*, he thought.

Last year, he and his mother had taken the family Holden on the 800-kilometre journey south to visit the university, stopping in Christchurch overnight with his grandparents on the way there and with family friends in Timaru on the way back. By the time they arrived home, his mother had mapped out his whole future. And as for his love life, she had quizzed him mercilessly.

"I just don't understand why you don't ask Holly out on a date. You spend most of your time with her," she had asked when they were waiting to board the ferry home. "It's obvious she likes you. You do know that, don't you?"

He had had to make up some excuse about not having the time right now, what with his exams and all. Eventually, she had conceded defeat and let the matter drop.

Perhaps you should just ask her out, he thought, *and get it over with.* Most of the guys in his year at college had already lost their virginity.

He let the prospectus drop into his lap, pushed himself up on his elbows and leaned his head against the wall. The television might as well have been in the same room; it was so loud. "Arsehole," he cursed under his breath.

Patch was sitting up, his tail thumping against the carpet, before Sam's own feet touched the floor. As Sam started across the room, towards the door, Patch stood to follow.

"Stay," he said as quietly but as authoritatively as he could. He pointed at the floor beside the bed. Patch let out a whine but lay down obediently. He rested his head on his paws and gave Sam a doleful look. "Good boy," he whispered and stepped out into the hall.

It was pitch-black, save for a thin strip of light below the living room door. He strained his ears for the sound of snoring, but all he could hear was the television.

Holding his breath, he slowly pushed the door ajar. The hinges creaked and he froze. He said a quick prayer that his father would be asleep.

He was in luck. Through the crack in the door, he could see his father's chair. His head had lolled forward onto his chest, and there was a large patch of drool on the front of his shirt. The stub of a roll-up cigarette clung to his lower lip and fluttered with each exhalation of breath.

He pushed the door open just enough to slip through, and keeping one eye on his father, tiptoed across the room to the television set. He made sure to step around the creaky floorboard by the rug. When his father grunted and shifted position in his seat, his heart almost stopped, but he kept going regardless.

His hands trembled as he reached for the volume control. Slowly, he turned the dial anticlockwise.

In hindsight, he should have stopped at muting the sound. Did it really matter if the television stayed on all night, so long as he couldn't hear it? Unfortunately, that thought didn't occur to him at the time. With a quick glance at his father, who was still sleeping like a baby, he flicked the power switch off.

There was a moment of pure, unadulterated silence. But then, as the components inside the television set began to cool, it made a series of loud cracking sounds. His father opened his eyes at once.

"What are you up to?" he growled, knocking the cigarette from his mouth.

Sam hesitated before answering. "I've got an exam in the morning, Dad," he said.

His father gripped the armrests and pushed himself to his feet with a grunt. He scratched at the stubble on his cheek. "What're you doing in here then?"

"I couldn't sleep with the TV on."

It was impossible to predict what mood his father would be in after he had been drinking. Sometimes he could be friendly, affectionate even; more often than not, he would come home spoiling for a fight.

"You think you're so much better than me, don't you?" his father growled, and his heart dropped. As his father took a step towards him, he took a step backwards.

"Where do you think you're going?" his father sneered. "You're just like your mother. You think you're so much better than the rest of us."

He refused to take the bait. There was no point in arguing when his father was in one of these moods. "Dad, I've got an exam in the morning," he said, very matter of fact.

His father's eyebrows drew together and his forehead furrowed. "I don't care if you've got a meeting with the bloody Queen."

His father was remarkably strong for a man of his age, and when he lunged forward and gripped his arm, it hurt like hell. "You can leave when I say you can leave." If his mother and sister weren't awake already, they would be now.

Up close, he could see the capillary veins in his father's face—a web of purple lines that testified to a life of heavy drinking.

"Maybe you shouldn't be going to university at all. What if I refuse to pay?" his father continued. He kept his mouth shut.

"Answer me when I'm talking to you," his father shouted, tightening his grip.

"Dad, I've got an exam tomorrow," he repeated. "Please can I go to bed?"

His father flung his arm away in disgust. "What do you want to go to university for anyway? You think you're so much better than me," his father repeated. This time he seemed to be speaking more to himself.

When his father backhanded him across the face, he was completely unprepared. He stumbled backwards and collided with the doorframe. A shooting pain shot through his skull as it thumped against the wood.

SAM

It took a moment for him to fully comprehend what had just happened. His father had never hit him before, though he knew he had come close to it several times.

"Get out of my sight," his father cursed and turned away.

Still in shock, he backed out of the room, pulling the door closed behind him.

He sat on the edge of the bed and touched his bottom lip. He could taste blood in the back of his mouth, warm and metallic. Patch padded over and gently nuzzled his elbow, but he pushed him away. He needed some space. He reached for the glass on his bedside table. His hands were still shaking and the water sloshed over the edge of the glass, onto the carpet.

The bedroom was freezing, and with its barely insulated walls and single-glazed sash window, he might as well have been sitting in the yard. Every exhalation of breath evaporated like a puff of white smoke.

He climbed back into bed and pulled the covers up under his chin but, ten minutes later, he was still shivering.

"Come on, boy," he whispered and patted the covers. The mattress dipped to one side as Patch clambered up onto the bed and lay down beside him, his large furry bulk providing some much needed warmth.

chapter four

SAM WAS STILL writing frantically when the invigilator called time. He scribbled down a few last words, placed the pen on the table, and sat back in his seat. It was over.

As soon as the last of the exam papers had been collected, he was up and heading for the door. Free at last, he wasn't going to spend a minute longer at school than he needed to. A voice called after him, but he pretended that he hadn't heard.

He took the stairs several steps at a time, shoved open the heavy metal door at the bottom, and stumbled out into the sunshine. As he crossed the field, towards the gates, he ran his tongue over the wound on his lower lip. The skin had already started to knit together. In a couple of days, it would be almost healed.

The Basin Reserve was still open to the public; another day, though, and it would be blocked off ahead of the upcoming test series against Australia. He entered via the southern gates and circumvented the oval. The grass was already yellowing in places. Several groundsmen were inspecting the wicket. Their hands were clasped behind their backs. They looked deep in conversation.

The dairy owner looked up as he entered the shop. "That time of day already, na?" he said, folding his newspaper and tucking it away beside the cash register. He nodded in reply.

"Twenty Marlboro, please," he said and dropped a crumpled-up note on the counter.

"Perfect weather for the cricket, na?" The dairy owner tried to make conversation. He turned and plucked a packet of cigarettes from the top shelf behind him. "Reckon we'll win?"

"No idea," Sam shrugged, pocketing the change.

He opened the packet, dropped the plastic wrapping into the bin outside, and removed a cigarette. He lit the end, inhaled, and flicked the smouldering match into the gutter. The dairy owner was right; the weather was perfect.

He didn't have time to hide when Sutcliffe walked around the corner. And, of course, Sutcliffe didn't fail to notice him immediately.

"G'day, gay boy," Sutcliffe called out. His voice carried across the street, to the café opposite. Several people looked in their direction. Sam took a deep breath and turned away. *Just ignore him*, he told himself. But giving up without getting a reaction wasn't Sutcliffe's style.

Something soft hit the back of his head, and he looked down to see a scrunched-up burger wrapper land at feet. Sutcliffe roared with laughter.

Adrenalin was surging around his body. All his instincts were telling him to flee, but he wouldn't give Sutcliffe the satisfaction. By sheer force of will, he crossed slowly to the other side of the road. Only then did he quicken his pace to put some distance between them.

The groundsmen were still hard at work when he arrived back at the cricket oval. He took a seat high up in one of the stands. It was chilly in the shade, and he pulled his jacket around his body.

Thank God he would be leaving soon. By this time next year, it would all be a memory. An unpleasant one, but a memory nonetheless. The thought was slightly comforting. *And perhaps I'll have got my shit together by then*, he wondered, but somehow he doubted it.

"So this is where you're hiding, gay boy?" He was lost in thought and didn't see Sutcliffe and his two sidekicks walk through the gate and up the steps. They were nearly upon him before he realised.

A malevolent grin spread across Sutcliffe's face. "Where's that girlfriend of yours today?" he laughed. "She gone looking for a real man?" Sutcliffe grabbed his crotch and made a lewd gesture with his tongue.

"Do one, why don't you," he replied. Sutcliffe folded his arms and perched on the back of the seat in front.

"That's not very nice, bro." Sutcliffe pretended to be offended. "Can't you take a joke?" He saw Sutcliffe wink out of the corner of his eye. One of the other guys sidled behind him. "Nice sunnies you got there," Sutcliffe continued.

He knew what was coming but he didn't have time to get to his feet. Two hands shot under his armpits and reached round the back of his neck, pinning him to the chair.

"Fuck off!" he shouted, trying to move his head, but

escape was impossible. Sutcliffe leaned in and plucked the glasses casually from his face.

"Not bad at all." Sutcliffe put the glasses on. His head was much wider than Sam's and the arms looked as if they were about to snap off. "A bit scratched, though," he said and dropped them on the floor. They made a horrid crunching sound as he stood on them.

"You fucking bastard," Sam cursed.

Sutcliffe stiffened and looked down at him. Clearly, he had hit a nerve. "What the fuck did you call me, you little shit?"

Sam's mouth seemed to acquire a life of its own. "You fucking arseholes," he screamed at his attackers, "I'll make you pay for that!"

When he opened his eyes, he was lying on his back on the cold, hard concrete. He gazed up at the corrugated roof of the grandstand. It took a second to remember where he was. Blood was streaming from his nose, into his mouth. The taste was becoming far too familiar for his liking.

He ran his tongue around his mouth, fearful of what he might find, but thankfully his teeth were all intact. The cut on his lip had burst open again, though, and already it had swollen to twice its normal size.

Sutcliffe and the others were long gone. Now it was the groundsmen who were staring at him. They all had concerned looks on their faces.

"You all right, son?" the oldest of the three men asked, helping him to his feet. "Are you hurt?"

He looked around, confused. Why were all his belongings on the ground? Were those his revision notes strewn across the pitch?

46

All of a sudden, he felt a wave of nausea surge up from inside. He sank to his knees and puked on the concrete.

"I think we ought to get you to hospital, son." The groundsman who had spoken before rested a hand on his shoulder, but he brushed it away.

He hauled himself to his feet again. "No, I'm fine," he mumbled, stooping to pick up his belongings and almost falling forward onto his face. A sharp pain shot through in his side as he twisted his body to right himself.

The other two groundsmen gathered his things and stuffed them back into his bag. They offered to take him to Accident and Emergency, but he refused point blank to go with them. Ignoring their protests, he limped over to the gate.

When he arrived home, he slipped into the house as quietly as he could manage, but his mother still heard the door open. "Sam, is that you?" she called out from the kitchen.

He took a deep breath before replying, "Yeah, it's me. I'm just going to have a shower before tea."

"Well, don't be long. It will be ready soon."

He took off his bloodstained shirt and threw it into the corner of the bathroom in disgust. Then he limped over to the mirror to inspect his face. It looked as bad as it felt.

As well as a fat lip, he had the beginnings of a black eye. Sutcliffe's blows had driven his lower lip into his teeth, puncturing the flesh, and the volley of punches to his abdomen had almost certainly broken a rib or two.

His mum almost dropped what she was holding when he walked into the kitchen. "What on earth happened to you?" she gasped. There was an almighty clang as she dropped the pan into the sink and rushed forward. She cupped his face in her hands. "Dear God, look at your nose."

As she reached out to touch it, he shrank from her hand, in anticipation of the pain.

"We need to get you to the hospital."

"I'm OK, Mum. It's nothing." He tried his best to sound as casual as possible, but he felt his voice breaking. Despite his best efforts, a tear broke free and ran down his cheek.

"Oh, Sam," his mother said. She put her arms around him. "John, come here," she called over his shoulder. The sound was like a knife stabbing through his skull, and he winced.

"What?" his father shouted back.

"Sam's been hurt. You're going to have to take him to the after-hours."

He extricated himself from his mother's arms and filled a glass with cold water from the tap.

"What's happened to you, then?" his father asked, appearing in the doorway.

"Nothing," he replied, avoiding his father's eye. He took a sip of water and immediately tasted blood again. He swished the water around his mouth and spat it out into the sink.

They drove to the medical centre and back in silence.

"Two broken ribs," his father announced as they walked through the front door. His mother pulled him up close and gripped him by the shoulders. She looked him straight in the eyes. "Who did this to you, Sam? I want you to tell me right now."

His father was standing behind him, but he could sense that he was waiting, listening, for his answer.

"Just leave it, Mum," he mumbled.

"This is no trivial matter," she scolded, her grip tightening. "The people who did this to you need to be punished. John, tell him he needs to tell us who did this." She reached up and touched the cut on his lip. Should he tell her that his father was partly to blame? He wasn't sure she'd want to know.

He was picking at his dinner when his mother walked back into the kitchen. She had been speaking with his father in the living room. "Make sure you eat it all up," she said, looking at the food he had barely touched.

"I'm not hungry, Mum."

She folded her arms and stared at him. He was looking down at his plate, but he could feel the intensity of her gaze.

"Well?" she said, after a long, awkward silence.

He shrugged. "I told you, it's nothing. I just got in a fight. That's all."

"Look at your face, Sam. I wouldn't call that nothing." She sighed and sat down opposite. "Are you being bullied?"

"No!" He shook his head and shovelled a forkful of mashed potato into his mouth before she could ask another question. He chewed slowly. "It was just a stupid fight," he said, grimacing as he swallowed. "It's nothing to stress about."

His mother opened her mouth to say something, but he cut her off by pushing his chair back from the table and getting to his feet.

"Sam—"

"I just need to lie down, Mum." He gave her shoulder a squeeze as he left the room. "I'll be fine—really."

Sitting on the edge of the bed, listening to his mother clattering about in the kitchen—the chink of china as she stacked the dishwasher; the scraping of chair legs on the floor as she swept around the table—he felt a pang of guilt in the pit of his stomach. He shouldn't have been so short with her. He knew she couldn't help but worry, and she had problems enough to contend with at the moment without his adding to them.

He reached down, picked up the university prospectus, which had fallen onto the floor the night before, and gazed at the faces smiling up at him from the cover. He threw the booklet across the room. It hit the wall with a thud and fell open on the carpet. He fell back onto the bed with a sigh.

It was pitch-black when he woke several hours later. He was still lying on top of the covers, and his hands and feet felt like blocks of ice. He staggered, half asleep, across the hall towards the bathroom, his bladder full to bursting.

He was making his way back to his bedroom when he noticed that the kitchen light was still on. No doubt his mother had left it on by accident. He stopped and turned towards the kitchen to switch it off.

The kitchen door was ajar. He couldn't see much except the pantry and a slither of the bench. The kitchen table was tucked away behind the door, hidden from view. As he reached through the gap, feeling along the wall for the light switch, a muffled sob pierced the silence.

He snatched back his hand and froze.

He had seen his mother upset plenty of times, but right now, he wasn't sure he had the energy to deal with whatever had happened. Still, he couldn't bring himself to leave her crying all by herself. He stepped forward and pushed open the door.

It was hard to say who was the more startled: him or his father.

His father jumped up from the table as if he had been caught with his hand in the till. He turned to face the wall.

"What are you playing at," his father growled, "creeping around the house in the middle of the night?"

He was lost for words. Never in his life had he seen his father cry; in fact, he didn't think his father was even capable of it. "Sorry, I—"

His father sniffed and wipe a hand under his nose. "This never happened—OK?"

THE SUN HADN'T been up for long when he climbed out of bed. He pulled on an old pair of track pants and a hoodie and crept across the room. Every movement hurt like hell. His head was still pounding, but he couldn't stay cooped up inside any longer. He snatched his sunglasses off the desk—an old pair he had found at the back of a drawer—and made his way quietly along the hall, towards the front door.

As he passed the kitchen, he glanced in. The room was empty, and for a fleeting moment he wondered whether last night had been a dream—a bad dream— but the pouch of rolling tobacco on the table confirmed otherwise. At some point during the night, Patch had moved from his usual spot at the foot of his bed and was now sprawled across the kitchen floor. The instant the front door clicked open, he was on his feet, his tail wagging.

"Shush," Sam said, snatching up Patch's lead. Patch had fetched it from the pantry and was dragging it behind him across the floor. The noise was loud enough to wake the dead. Patch squeezed past him and out the door.

It had been raining on and off all night, and dark storm clouds were now rolling up from the south. It would be pouring within the hour. He pulled the hood over his head and half-walked, half-limped out onto the footpath. "Come on then," he said, giving the lead a yank.

Every inhalation of breath sent a stabbing pain up under his ribcage and brought tears to his eyes. The doctor had told him there was nothing he could do to make his ribs heal faster; it was simply a matter of letting nature take its course. Still, the doctor had given him strict instructions to rest.

He took a deep breath, winced, and continued on, towards the ocean. Anything was better than waiting around the house for his parents to wake up. He would give his father a wide berth for a couple of days.

When they reached the foreshore, he turned right, past the surf club and the half a dozen surf lifesavers hauling kayaks out of the shed onto the sand. The seagulls squawked angrily overhead, swooping and soaring on the wind, as he and Patch passed by. The waves were crashing against the rocks at the eastern end of the beach, exploding one after the other in bursts of white foam.

He cupped his hands in front of his face and breathed into his palms until the warmth of his breath defrosted his nose and cheeks.

Despite the early hour and the darkening sky, the beach was far from deserted. A hundred or so metres away, two dogs were chasing each other back and forth through the ankle-deep water. Patch pulled on the lead, eager to join in, but he had no intention of stopping. "Come on, boy," he said, pulling him reluctantly in the opposite direction.

By the time they reached the rugby club close to his house, the rain had set in well and truly. He lit a cigarette and took shelter beneath the eaves of the clubhouse while Patch, happy to be off the lead at last, sniffed around the goal posts at the far end of the pitch. When he found the perfect spot, he cocked his hind leg and urinated.

Patch was making his way back across the field, nose down, tail wagging, when the double doors on his right swung open and a mass of bodies spilled out into the fresh air.

"Crowd around, boys." The players formed a tight circle around their coach. It was bitterly cold, and it looked as if they all had smoke billowing from the tops of their heads.

He pressed his back against the wall and watched as they began their training.

His father had wanted so much for him to be good at sport. As soon as he was old enough, he had signed him up for the junior rugby team and the junior soccer team. New kit, new boots—his father had bought the whole caboodle. He even had his mother stitch his surname onto the back of his jersey.

Where are you going, boy? Open your bloody eyes! That type of encouragement might have worked with other boys, but with him it had had the opposite effect. The constant criticism made him only more self-conscious. After just two seasons, his jersey had been retired for good.

He stubbed out his cigarette on the wall and was turning to leave when he caught a glimpse of a familiar face in the group. It was Patch's victim from the beach.

The players were working their way from one end of the pitch to the other, catching and passing the ball between them. He watched, mesmerised, as the ball flew from one pair of hands straight into the next. They made it look effortless, and he felt a pang of jealousy.

When the players reached the end of the pitch closest to the clubhouse, the coach blew on his whistle and gestured for everybody to crowd around. The rain was coming down hard now, and the players huddled close to each other. The guy from the beach was standing at the edge of the pack, his hands on his hips. Water was pouring from his wavy hair, and his jersey, saturated already, clung to his body.

After a short pep talk, the players divided into groups for scrum practice.

Sam tried not to stare too overtly, but he couldn't keep his eyes off the blond-haired stranger, who stepped forward and locked arms with the two props on either side of him. A second and a third row fell in behind, and at the coach's command, the two front rows crouched and touched shoulders.

"Engage!" the coach shouted over the ruckus and the two halves of the scrum came together with a thud. But within a matter of seconds the pack buckled under its own weight and collapsed in on itself. "Get up and try it again."

The next attempt was more successful, and he watched, his eyes glued on the centre of the pack, as the two teams pushed against each other. Blond-haired's jersey was pulled taut over his back, and the tendons in his forearms bulged as he gripped the players on either side of him. Sixteen pairs of studded boots chewed into the muddy pitch as each team tried to force the other backwards, towards an imaginary try line.

He wasn't paying any attention to the ball and didn't notice when it emerged from the back of the scrum. One of the other players darted forward and scooped it up. He turned and punted it fifty metres down the field.

Patch was sniffing the grass at the side of the pitch. His ears pricked up.

"Stay!" he hissed, stepping towards Patch and reaching for his collar, but he wasn't quick enough, and Patch wriggled away. Before he could make another grab for him, Patch dropped back on his hind legs and then launched himself after the ball.

The oval ball spun as it sailed through the air. When it hit the ground, it bounced several times before finally wobbling to a stop. Patch was travelling too fast and overshot the mark. He tumbled to a stop, turned and scrambled back to the ball.

"Get that ball off that bloody dog," the coach's voice boomed across the field. But Patch had already sunk his teeth into the leather and was carrying it away into the bushes.

"Fucking dog," Sam cursed and chased after him as fast as his ribs would allow.

He found Patch hiding behind the large pohutukawa tree next to the clubhouse, and as he stepped towards him, Patch's ears went back. He let out a low, rumbling growl.

"Drop!" he ordered and made a grab for the drool-soaked leather. But instead of releasing his grip, Patch dropped forward onto his front legs and inched backwards. He was a large, powerful dog, and had no intention of losing this tug of war. He shook his head from side to side to try to loosen Sam's grip.

The jerking movement sent a sharp pain shooting through his body, and he yelped, letting go his grip. "Have it your way, then," he snapped, clutching his side and inhaling through his nose. As he turned to leave, Patch dropped the ball and looked up at him. He cocked his head, as if to ask why the game was over.

Sam's mother was sitting at the breakfast table when they arrived home. Her eyes were closed and she had her hands folded neatly in her lap.

He let Patch off the lead, kicked off his trainers and wandered into the room. His feet were steaming and left sweaty footprints on the grey slate tiles.

He buttered himself a piece of toast and flicked through the morning paper while his mother finished her morning prayers.

"You ask for the same things every day," his father scoffed as he walked into the kitchen and sat down. The sound of the chair legs as they scraped against the floor set his teeth on edge. "Couldn't you ask to win Lotto once in a while?"

His mother didn't react.

"Where have you been?" His father turned his attention to him.

"Walking the dog."

"The lawns need mowing today, and you can weed-eat the drive. You might as well make yourself useful now that you've finished school." His father slurped on his tea and reached across the table for the newspaper.

Although Sam had finished his toast, he was still hungry. He had hardly eaten anything the night before and now his stomach felt as if his throat had been cut. He rummaged through the pantry for something, anything, to eat and found a couple of Weet-Bix hiding at the bottom of a box. He put them in a bowl and poured over the last dribble of milk in the carton.

"Did you hear me?"

"Yes, Dad," he answered. "Mum, have we got any more milk?"

His mother closed her Bible and reached across the table for the teapot. "No, I'm afraid that was the last of it." She poured herself a cup of tea and added a spoonful of honey. She always drank hers black.

He added a dash of cold water to the Weet-Bix, and just enough sugar to disguise the soggy cardboard taste. He sat back down at the table and shovelled a spoonful of the grey mush into his mouth. It tasted as bad as it looked but he finished the bowl.

"Bloody pervert," his father muttered under his breath.

"What was that, John?"

His father pointed to the story on the front page of the paper: *Eastern ward elects first gay councillor.*

"This city is going to the dogs. Mark my words: it won't be long before they're running the joint."

In the space of a few seconds, Sam had gone from feeling hungry to wanting to be sick. He kept his eyes down and sipped his tea in silence.

"It's the way the world is going, John," his mother said. "Jesus said it would only get worse."

"Well, you can tell Jesus that I blame the parents," his father continued, looking up from his newspaper and draining his cup. He stood up and tossed the paper onto the table. "I'm going to work," he grunted. "Sam, don't forget those lawns."

He had been trying to read for the past hour, but he just couldn't concentrate. Interesting as the book was, he found he had to read every sentence twice—three times even—just to remember what was going on. He finally conceded defeat, folded down the corner of the page, and returned the book to the bedside table. Unopposed, his mind wandered back to the rugby field. He had seen the guy with the blond hair twice and spoken to him just once—hell, he didn't even know his name—yet he couldn't think of anything else.

The bedroom door was closed, but it wasn't locked. He knew that anybody could walk in and catch him, yet he couldn't stop himself. He undid the first few buttons of his jeans and slid a hand beneath the waist of his undies. It didn't take long for him to come. When his mother knocked on the door ten minutes later, he was already gazing out the window again.

"Sam, are you in there?" she called through the closed door.

He pushed himself up on his elbows and grabbed the book from the bedside table, opening it at random. He coughed to clear his throat. "Yes, I'm just reading."

The door opened a crack and his mother peered in. "Don't forget to mow the grass," she smiled.

Only then did he notice, to his absolute horror, that his pants were still undone. He rested the book across his lap and prayed that she wouldn't come into the room.

"Your father will be home soon," she continued.

He glanced at the clock on the bedside table. It was half past four already. *Shit, shit, shit.*

"Are you OK?"

"Eh?"

"You don't look very well," his mother said, stepping into the room, to his horror. She walked over to his desk and picked up a dirty cup and plate.

"No, I'm fine," he said, trying to smile naturally. *Please, please go away.*

She gave him a long, penetrating look, turned and walked out of the room, closing the door behind her.

He had only just wheeled the lawnmower back to the garage when his father came striding up the path and disappeared into the house.

WHITE QUEEN TO G4. Check.

He rotated the chessboard carefully so as not to dislodge any of the pieces. Nevertheless, one of the pawns fell on its side and rolled across the carpet. He caught it and set it back in its rightful place. He stared, unblinking, at the chequered squares, sizing up each possible move.

Finally, satisfied he had thought of every alternative, he slid his last remaining bishop diagonally across the board. When he withdrew his hand, he noticed that the mitre had made an indentation in the tip of his index finger. He massaged it with his thumb and then rotated the board back through one hundred and eighty degrees, ready to counter the move he had just made.

"Sam, get that, will you?" his father said when the doorbell rang.

He hauled himself to his feet and stretched, his joints cracking like an old man's. A tear escaped from the corner of his eye and ran down his cheek. He wiped it away with his sleeve. As he passed the mirror in the hall, he glanced at his reflection. The bruise beneath his eye was darker still. It was obvious he had taken a fist to the face. He licked his fingers and tried to flatten down the cow's lick at the front of his head, but the unruly tuft of hair refused to stay down.

He opened the door and did a double take. The last person in the world he had been expecting to see was the blond stranger from the beach. His jaw almost hit the floor.

"Not you again!" the guy said, but his mouth turned up at the corners. A lock of blond hair fell down over one eye and he pushed it back behind his ear. "John Wilson lives here, right?"

He nodded his head. He could feel the blood rushing

to his face already. He almost tripped over his own feet as he moved to the side.

"Is that you, Tom?" his father shouted from the living room. "Come on through."

Tom. He made a mental note of the name.

"About the other day," Tom said, squeezing past, into the house, "I was already in a really bad mood—"

He was about to say "Don't worry about it" when Patch came bounding out of the kitchen. He threw himself at Tom's feet and let out a long, strangulated howl.

"Hey, mischief," Tom said, squatting on his heels. Patch was writhing around on the floor like some demented creature. He flipped onto all fours and nuzzled against Tom and sent him toppling backwards onto his bum.

"Sorry about him," Sam apologised, pulling Patch away and forcing him into the kitchen. He shut the door so that he couldn't escape.

Laughing, Tom removed his work boots and left them by the door.

It was clear that Tom had come straight from a job. His forearms were spattered with plaster, and the back of his T-shirt was damp between the shoulder blades.

Contractors often called by the house—his father had run his own building firm for years—but none of them had ever looked like Tom. Most of the subbies who worked for his father were middle-aged and had receding hairlines.

"Follow me," Sam said, and led Tom into the living room.

He returned to his seat on the floor, in front of the chessboard, while Tom perched on the edge of the sofa, opposite his father, and scribbled down his instructions for the morning.

"You know you can win in two moves, right?"

Tom's voice startled him. He hadn't realised Tom was looking in his direction. Tom put down the pad and reached for the board. "Do you mind?"

He shook his head.

Tom proceeded to move one of the white rooks three squares to the right. "Check," Tom said and grinned proudly.

Out of the corner of his eye, Sam could see his father watching them.

Now there was only one move possible. While Tom watched, he moved the black Queen.

Tom moved straight in for the kill with an opposing knight. "Checkmate."

They were both contemplating the board in silence when Sam's father interrupted with a cough. "You ready then?"

Tom nodded and disappeared to put his boots on. His father stayed where he was, though. He had an odd look on his face—as if there was something he wanted to say, but he couldn't quite find the words. There was a long, awkward silence before he finally said, "We're going to the golf club for a drink. Come with us if you want."

The clubhouse was exactly as he remembered it, although the yellow, nicotine-stained walls had received a fresh coat of paint. As they walked through the entrance, into the foyer, Tom veered off to the left.

"I'll see you both in there," Tom called over his shoulder and disappeared into the pro shop. Reluctantly,

Sam followed his father up the stairs to the bar.

"Two jugs of your finest," his father shouted across the bar, before making a beeline for his buddies. They were propping up a leaner in the corner. Ngaire, the duty manager, hopped down from her stool and limped over to the taps.

He had always remembered Ngaire as a force to be reckoned with—she had given him a dressing down once that had reduced him to tears—but now she looked more like an old lady. Her face had softened with age, and when she smiled, he noticed that half her teeth were missing. "G'day, son," she smiled. "You John's boy, eh?"

He nodded and handed over the money his father had given him to pay for the drinks.

"That'll be ten bucks," she mumbled. The tattoo on her chin had faded to turquoise, the intricate design of the tribal moko distorted by her wizened skin. She was smoking a cigarette, and it dangled precariously from her lips while she spoke. A centimetre of ash dropped from the tip and landed on the bar.

He carried the jugs over to his father's table, taking care not to slosh any beer on the carpet. He poured himself a glass and took a seat facing the door. From where Sam was sitting, he could see the entrance to the shop. He kept one eye on the door as he sipped on his drink.

Thirty minutes later, Tom still hadn't appeared.

"Go get another jug in, will you?" his father said, addressing him directly for the first time since they had arrived.

His mind was elsewhere, and he stared back, uncomprehending.

"Another jug," his father repeated and waved a lime-green banknote under his nose. Grudgingly, he got to his feet and traipsed back over to the bar. If he'd known he would have to spend the evening alone with his father and his cronies, he would have made up an excuse to stay home.

He was standing in line, waiting to be served, when Tom finally emerged from the pro shop. He felt his spirits climb and then immediately plummet. Tom had a look of thunder on his face. Instead of continuing on to the bar, he turned and headed back towards the car park.

"Here, I'm just going to the loo," he told his father, placing the jug and the change on the table, and headed out into the lobby. He reached the sliding glass doors just in time to see Tom's truck pull out of the car park and disappear.

chapter five

SAM HAD SPENT every Saturday morning for the past six months stacking shelves and packing bags at the local supermarket. The work was mind-numbingly boring, and it didn't pay much—in fact, his parents had stopped his allowance the moment he got the job, which meant he was now only marginally better off than he'd been before—but it gave him an excuse to get out of the house.

"Hey, Wilson, need a lift?" Lloyd, a lad he knew from school, who also worked the Saturday morning shift, called out to him across the car park.

"Nah, I'm good, thanks," he replied. It was a nice day, if slightly muggy, and the sun was shining. He was in no rush to get home, especially now that he had no revision to consider.

He heard the motorbike before he saw it. It came roaring around the corner, shot straight past him and carried on up the street for several hundred metres before doing a U-turn. The rider, crouched low over the handlebars, flew back along the road and screeched to a halt alongside him. After what had happened at the Basin Reserve, his first instinct was to run, but logic told him he had no chance of outrunning a bike.

"I thought it was you," the rider said, pushing up his visor.

He recognised Tom instantly, even though only his eyes and the bridge of his nose were visible. A strand of blond hair had escaped from beneath Tom's helmet and was hanging down over his right eye.

He pulled the headphones from his ears and let the cords hand around his neck. The music continued to play, indistinct and tinny.

"Hi," he replied, trying his best to appear cool. Relieved though he was not to find himself face to face with Sutcliffe, his heart continued to pound against the inside of his chest.

"So you ride a bike," he said, blurting out the first inanity that came into his head. He wanted to kick himself as soon as the words were out of his mouth.

"Yeah, she's my baby," Tom laughed and patted the engine affectionately, "Where are you off to?"

"Just home," he replied. His tongue felt awkward in his mouth, as if he were trying to speak a language he didn't know. "I've just finished work."

"I was just going for a ride. Do you want to come?"

He didn't answer straight away. He had never been on a bike before, and although he didn't suppose riding pillion was inherently difficult, he wasn't in a rush to make a fool of himself, either.

"Go on," Tom encouraged, "I'll go gently."

Mum would flip out if she knew I was even entertaining the idea, he thought. But Holly was always telling him he needed to be more spontaneous—more open to new experiences. He swallowed and said, "OK, thanks," before he could change his mind.

He took a step towards the bike and stopped. "Wait, I don't have a helmet."

Tom didn't seem bothered by the news. "Stay here," he said and, with a twist of the throttle, roared off up the road. He was back within a few minutes.

"Here, this should fit." Tom handed him a matt black helmet. It had a deep scratch across the brow and looked as if it had seen better days. "It's my spare," Tom explained, as if reading his thoughts.

He held the helmet in both hands and peered into its close, padded interior. The cavity looked far too small; much too narrow for his head.

At first, the helmet seemed to fit OK, but when it reached his ears, it wouldn't go any further. "I think it's too small," he mumbled beneath the padding. His eyes and nose were completely enclosed and he could feel his claustrophobia beginning to kick in. He pulled down on the helmet, but it wouldn't budge.

Before he knew it had happened, one well-placed thump on the top of his head sent the helmet sliding past his ears and into place.

"There you go!" Tom lifted the visor covering Sam's face and smiled. "Come on. Jump on the back." He revved the engine a couple of times for effect.

The whole bike wobbled as he held on to Tom and swung himself up onto the seat. "Sorry!" he shouted over Tom's shoulder, releasing his death grip on Tom's jacket.

He didn't think to put his visor down, and as they flew

along the main drag to the city, he had to keep his head turned to the side to shield his eyes. When they rounded the bend at the top of Wellington Road, fear trumped embarrassment, and he wrapped his arms around Tom's waist.

The road was clear in the opposite direction, and Tom swung the bike out into the right-hand lane to overtake a long line of cars. They darted back across the median strip just in time to avoid an oncoming truck. *So much for going gently*, he thought.

He had no idea where they were heading or how long they would be gone, but he couldn't have cared less. He had never felt so exhilarated in his life.

When they stopped at the traffic lights on the other side of the tunnel, he relaxed his grip slightly—although he didn't let go altogether. Adrenalin was coursing through his body and his legs were shaking uncontrollably. He hoped Tom wouldn't notice.

It wasn't long before the city was behind them and they were snaking their way through the hills of the south coast. The road was narrow in places, and every time a car came towards them, he held his breath and closed his eyes, anticipating a collision that, fortunately, never came. The sky, a perfect blue only an hour before, was growing darker by the minute, and the first drops of rain fell as they reached the stony beach at Ohariu Bay.

"Quick, it's about to piss down," Tom yelled over his shoulder, kicking the motorbike's stand into place. His peripheral vision was obstructed by the helmet and he had to turn his head a full ninety degrees to check whether the road was clear. He needn't have bothered, though; the beach was completely deserted.

The gravel crunched underfoot as they ran towards the ramshackle café, which appeared to be closed. The door was ajar, however.

"Hello?" Sam called out, stepping inside, out of the rain. Tom followed closed behind him. As if in reply, a flash of lightning ripped across the sky and they both jumped backwards.

"You get a shock?" Tom laughed, pushing him forward into the room. The rain was coming down hard and it was truly deafening, the sound it made as it pummelled the corrugated iron roof.

He had to ask Tom to help him again, this time to remove the helmet. Tom's fingers brushed his skin as he gripped the helmet under the base and tugged. For a moment, nothing happened, and then his head popped free. His hands went straight to his ears, to check that they were still attached.

A light flicked on in the back room and a nervous-looking girl peeked around the doorway. "Can I help you?"

His head felt as light as a feather without the helmet—as if it might float off his shoulders. "Are you open?" he asked.

The girl nodded and turned on the main lights. He saw the muscles in her face relax and wondered what, or whom, she had been expecting. "Take a seat, and I'll bring some menus over."

The plastic awning was already beginning to sag under the weight of the rain pooling between the wooden beams. In one corner, a steady stream of water was pouring through a tear in the plastic, soaking the concrete floor below.

They took a seat in the far corner, which was still relatively dry. The waitress appeared a moment later, two laminated menus held in front of her like a shield. "Can I get you anything to drink?"

He gave the grubby menu a cursory glance and ordered a trim flat white. Tom asked for the same, handing his menu back without even looking at it. "And some hot chips."

"Just the one?"

"Nah, a bowl would be nice." Tom winked at the waitress, but she didn't smile back. She scurried away to the kitchen, leaving them alone.

He didn't jump at the second flash of lightning, although he did start to count in his head. *One Mississippi, two Mississippi, …*

"It's getting closer," Tom said, as if reading his thoughts.

He nodded and looked out at the rain, which was coming down so fast it looked more like night-time outside than early afternoon. "Have you been here before?" he asked, changing the subject.

"Yeah, I come every year," Tom replied, but he didn't offer up any more information. Instead, he licked the end of his finger and rubbed a speck of dirt from the sleeve of his jacket.

They sat in silence until their coffees arrived. The sugar sachets were damp and the sugar fell out in clumps.

Tom had finished half his drink before he spoke again. "It's ten years today since my dad died. He's buried up on the hill."

Tom sat forward and rested his elbows on the table. He lowered his voice slightly. "Sorry about the other night— about leaving without saying goodbye. It was my sister. She was having a meltdown. It's the same every year."

"Don't worry about it." He wanted to ask what had happened to their father but thought it might be insensitive. Tom didn't offer up the information, in any case. "Your mum," he said, changing the subject, "does she live in Wellington?"

Tom shook his head. "Thank God. She's down south with her new husband. We don't exactly get along."

The rain was beginning to let up by the time their chips arrived, and the leak in the roof had slowed to a steady drip. The waitress disappeared, returning a minute later with salt, pepper, and a half-empty glass bottle, smeared with congealed tomato sauce.

"You have it," he said when they were down to the last chip. He pushed the bowl across the table. Tom picked up the chip, took a bite, and handed him the other half.

He tried his best not to smile, but he couldn't help himself. "Thanks." He wiped his greasy fingers on a paper napkin and got to his feet. "So did you want to visit the cemetery then?"

Tom looked surprised. "Only if you don't mind."

"Of course not."

As he reached for his wallet, Tom held up a hand and said, "It's on me."

He tried to protest, but Tom wouldn't have a bar of it.

The storm had moved on up the coast, leaving a crisp, refreshed landscape in its wake. All the humidity had evaporated from the air.

"Are you sure you don't mind?" Tom asked again, slipping into his jacket and zipping up the front as they walked back across the car park, towards the bike.

He shook his head. "No, it's absolutely fine. Take as long as you like. I'm in no rush to get home." In fact, he had an aunt buried up there too. He really ought to visit her, but he didn't like to admit that he didn't know where her grave was.

Just as they reached the bike, he had an idea. Without saying a word, he turned and jogged across the street, towards the cluster of houses opposite the café. Tom called after him, but he continued as if he hadn't heard.

At the very end of the row, facing out over the pebbled beach, was an old bach. Its blue weatherboard exterior had clearly seen better days, and its corrugated iron roof was orange with rust. It was beginning to lift on one side; the next strong southwesterly would probably peel it back like the lid on a tin of sardines.

The curtains were drawn and the driveway was empty. There were weeds growing through multiple cracks in the concrete. Clearly, nobody had been home for quite some time.

Along the fence line, a row of agapanthus was in full bloom; long green stalks protruded from the ground at varying angles, their blue and white funnel-shaped flowers dripping with fresh rainwater.

He crouched down, glanced around to check that nobody was watching, and quickly snapped off half a dozen stems. Tom didn't say a word as Sam walked back across the car park, the makeshift bouquet clutched to his chest, but there was the hint of a smile on his face.

Tom knew exactly where he was going and brought the bike to a stop at the north end of the cemetery, beneath the shade of a large Norfolk pine.

He hung back, not wanting to intrude, but as Tom stepped carefully between the graves, he called over his shoulder, "They won't bite, you know," and motioned for him to follow.

Tom stopped at a small square plaque several rows back from the road and knelt on the grass. He brushed away a couple of leaves that had fallen onto the headstone.

"My sister's been already," he said, nodding at the small bunch of flowers that had been placed on the grave.

"Here," he said, handing down the flowers he had picked. He felt rather foolish now; the agapanthus looked pitiful compared with Tom's sister's red and white roses. But Tom didn't seem to notice. He moved his sister's flowers to one side and gently laid Sam's beside them.

"Thanks for coming with me." Tom looked up at him and smiled. He touched the plaque one last time and got to his feet. "You know, I'd just turned thirteen when he died."

They took a step towards the road.

"Sometimes I find it hard to remember his voice. I can see him, clear as anything, but his voice escapes me."

When they reached the bike, Tom looked back at the grave one last time. He had a strange expression on his face—as if he were trying to solve a cryptic crossword or some equally difficult puzzle. Sam waited in silence until Tom was ready to leave.

"Let's get out of here, eh?" Tom hopped up onto the bike and kicked the engine into life.

As soon as he walked through the door, he knew that somebody—his mother—had been in his room. The clothes that he had left in a heap on the floor were stacked in a neat pile on his bed. The empty glasses were missing from his desk, too, and the chest that he was filling with things to take to Dunedin had been pushed against the wall.

Patch was lying in his usual spot. He opened one eye, wagged his tail half-heartedly, and went back to sleep.

He rushed over to the bed, dropped to his knees, and lifted the mattress.

"Fuck," he cursed, slumping back on his heels in complete disbelief. He had bought the magazine only a few days before, at a dairy on the other side of the city. He had carried it to the counter, concealed beneath a newspaper. He had barely been able to look at the dairy owner as he handed over the money. He hadn't waited for his change.

He lifted the mattress again and took a second look, thinking—hoping—that the magazine had fallen between the slats, but it wasn't on the floor. A quick search under the bed netted nothing but an odd sock and a discarded chewing gum wrapper.

He pushed himself to his feet and perched, stunned, on the edge of the desk. His pulse was hammering in his ears, so much so that the traffic outside sounded a mile away. A trickle of cold sweat escaped his hairline and ran down his temple. He reached down, grabbed the waste paper basket, and vomited.

Once he had finished being sick, he wiped his mouth on his sleeve and took a deep breath.

Look, you haven't broken the law, he told himself. But he knew that excuse wouldn't carry any weight with his mother. He would have to tell her that somebody else had put it there. Owning up simply wasn't an option.

His mother was standing at the sink when he walked into the kitchen. She finished peeling the potato in her hand and dropped it into a pan of salted water on the stovetop. She dried her hands on a tea towel and turned around. It was obvious that she had been crying. Her eyes were all red and puffy. He looked down at the floor, like some badly behaved child.

"It's not mine," he said. The words seemed to come out of his mouth all by themselves. "It's not mine."

His mother didn't say a word. Instead, she turned away and plunged her hands back into the water. She set to work on another potato, staring straight ahead, as if she were searching for something amongst the flowers in the front yard.

"Whose is it then?" she asked at last. He didn't know how to answer the question, so he stayed silent. "I thought I'd brought you up better than that."

She turned to face him again. This time, she let her arms hang at her side. Water dripped from her fingertips onto the floor.

"Holly," he said. He felt a pang of guilt as he said her name, but it was the first one he thought of.

"Holly?" his mother repeated, her voice several octaves higher.

"Yeah, she thought it'd be funny to put it in my bag. You know, on the last day of term. A whole heap of us got pranked. I couldn't exactly put it in the kitchen bin, though," he said defensively, "so I hid it under the bed."

She gave him an intense look. He knew that she was weighing up the story. What he had told her was possible yet unlikely, but, clearly, she wanted to believe. It was better than accepting the alternative. She dropped onto the nearest chair with a sigh.

"Oh, Sam," she stifled a laugh, "I didn't know what to think. Honestly, I didn't." She shook her head and her face grew serious again. "But to think that you could bring something like that into the house."

The awkward silence that followed was broken by the shrill ring of the doorbell.

He gasped when he opened the front door. The blood that had only just begun to return to his cheeks drained away again.

"Want a pineapple lump?" Holly asked, and thrust a crumpled brown paper bag under his nose. The sickly sweet smell of the lollies turned his stomach. "You look a bit pale. Are you OK?"

"I'm fine," he answered. He glanced towards the kitchen—his mother had her head in the pantry—and pushed Holly out into the front yard. He closed the door quietly behind him. "Let's get out of here, eh?" he said, pulling her away from the house, towards the street.

"Hey, what's going on?" she protested. "Are you sure you're OK? I heard what happened."

He stopped dead in his tracks. "What?"

"Your mum told my mum what happened," Holly

said, her mouth full of chocolate, "and then my mum told me, of course."

"My mum told your mum," he repeated. He couldn't believe what he was hearing. Holly nodded.

"She told her what exactly?"

Holly looked at him, her eyebrows drawn together. "About the attack, of course."

She popped another lolly into her mouth and started towards the road. "Do you fancy going to the movies? I'll protect you if we bump into Sutcliffe," she added with a smirk.

"I can't, sorry," he replied, distracted. His father was walking along the street, towards them. "Dinner is nearly ready, so I'd better get back inside. I'll catch you tomorrow, eh?"

Holly shrugged and walked off in the other direction.

He shut himself away in his room after tea. He wasn't sure he could face any more questions from his mother. Thankfully, his sister was staying the night at a friend's house and his father had disappeared to the golf club. His mother must have felt the same as he did, because she disappeared into her room and didn't come out for the rest of evening.

He pulled the duvet up around his neck, against the icy draught that was stealing in through cracks in the window frame. The wind had been gaining in strength all day and was now howling around the eaves. He had been reading for the past two hours, but he couldn't keep his eyes open for another second.

He knew exactly why Holly had invited him to the movies. It was the second time in a week that she had suggested they hang out. It was becoming increasingly difficult to think of excuses. He thought he had made it clear that he wasn't interested in her as anything more than a mate, but, evidently, the message still hadn't got through.

He was just drifting off when his cellphone vibrated against top of the bedside table. The noise was loud enough to wake the dead.

It was pitch-black with the light off, and when he flipped open the cover on the phone, the fluorescent glare of the screen stabbed at his corneas. He clamped his eyes shut and let a few seconds pass before he tried to open them again.

Hey Sam, we're having a party if you're interested?

He didn't recognise the number, and it wasn't saved against any of the contacts in his phone. He decided to wait for a while before replying. If it was Holly, he would have to think carefully about what he wrote.

A couple of minutes later, the little envelope icon appeared again. He propped himself up on one elbow and stared at the screen.

Ha! sorry bro, it's Tom.

He leaned over, flicked on the bedside lamp, and read the message several more times. No, he wasn't imagining it. It was definitely from Tom.

For a moment, he wondered whether Tom had messaged him by mistake, but then he remembered that the invitation had been addressed to him in person.

A third message came through a few seconds later— this time, with Tom's address. He threw back the covers and flew out of bed. In his haste to get dressed, he almost forgot to reply.

Thanks, I'll be there soon, he messaged back, sitting down on the end of the bed to tie his laces.

He was almost ready to leave when his father arrived home. The force with which the front door flew open sent a shockwave reverberating through the whole house.

He stopped where he was and held his breath. Hopefully, his father would be too drunk to notice the thin strip of light beneath his bedroom door.

There was a long silence, followed by the chinking of glasses. He recognised the sound immediately. In a few moments, his father would stagger past, a cut-glass tumbler in one hand and a bottle of scotch in the other. If Patch was unfortunate enough to be sleeping in the hall, he would probably get a kick for good measure.

Fuck you, he cursed, backing away from the door as quietly as he could. He would have to leave via the window. The wooden sash squeaked against the interior casing as he forced it open. As soon as the gap was wide enough, he squeezed through and made his escape.

Sam climbed the wooden steps to the upstairs flat and knocked on the frosted pane in the door. His heart was pounding and his mouth was uncomfortably dry. He ran his tongue over his lips and cupped his hands over his nose and mouth to check his breath.

An eternity seemed to pass before the dark silhouette of a person appeared behind the glass. Sam sucked in a deep breath, stood up straight, and squared his shoulders.

An exceptionally tall man with a fuzzy red beard

opened the door. He was holding a cigarette, which smelled suspiciously like marijuana. "You smoke?" he said, offering the joint across the threshold.

This was something that Sam hadn't prepared for. He shook his head, feeling more than a little bewildered. "Sorry."

The man in front of him had to be at least two metres tall. And judging by the breadth of his shoulders, he couldn't weigh any less than a hundred and twenty kilos.

"This is Tom's place, right?" Sam asked, suddenly fearing that he might have got the wrong apartment.

"Yeah, bro," the guy replied, taking a puff on the cigarette. His pupils were fully dilated, and he seemed to be having some trouble focusing. "You smoke?" he asked again.

Sam smiled and shook his head.

Inside the flat, the air was thick with smoke. Before he reached the end of the hallway, he was coughing up his lungs.

He wandered slowly from room to room. A few faces he recognised from college, but the vast majority he had never seen before.

Tom was in the kitchen, playing cards with a small group of friends.

"Full house, boys," howled the guy sitting opposite Tom, fanning his cards out on the table. Tom sighed and tossed his own hand into the centre. He pushed his chair back from the table and got to his feet.

"Sam," Tom said, spotting him standing in the doorway. He walked straight over. "You came."

When Tom smiled, Sam felt his insides turn to jelly. He nodded and looked away. "Nice place you've got here."

Tom looked around the room, as if seeing it for the first time too. "Yeah, it's OK, I guess," he said and shrugged his shoulders. He motioned towards the hall. "Come, we'll get you something to drink."

He followed Tom into the bathroom, where the tub had been turned into a makeshift chilly bin. Tom reached into the slush of ice cubes and plucked out two bottles of beer. He prised off the caps with the base of a lighter and handed him one of the bottles.

"Thanks," he said. "It's a pretty good location here."

Tom's eyebrows drew together.

"The flat," he explained. "It's close to town." He wanted to kick himself.

"Yeah," Tom smiled and held up his bottle. "Cheers."

The sky was already brightening in the east by the time the crowded apartment began to thin out. Sam looked at his watch and then at the clock on the living room wall. It felt as if he had only just arrived; and yet several hours had passed.

"Time to go, fellas," he heard Tom tell the stragglers in the kitchen. The sound of chair legs scraping against the linoleum floor made him wince. The voices moved along the hallway and then trailed off into the distance.

A peaceful silence descended on the flat and Sam was tempted to close his eyes. But instead, he got to his feet. He had no intention of outstaying his welcome either. But before he had finished buttoning up his jacket, Tom appeared in the doorway.

"Nightcap?" Tom said, holding up a bottle of whisky.

In his other hand, he was holding two cut-glass tumblers.

Sam had never drunk spirits neat before but he accepted the triple pour with a smile. Anything to put off leaving. He waited for Tom to take a sip, though, before he raised the glass to his lips.

As soon as the whisky touched the back of his throat, he thought was going to choke.

"You OK?" Tom laughed, taking the glass out of his hand and slapping him hard on the back. Tears were streaming down his face.

"I'm—fine—really," he spluttered, wiping his eyes with his hands. Once he was able to breathe again, Tom handed him back his drink.

He sat down on the sofa and leaned his head against the cushion.

A car rumbled past the open window. Its headlights illuminated the wall opposite for a few seconds. Sam attempted to focus on the swirling pattern, but the effort made him feel queasy. He stopped and closed his eyes. He had clearly drunk too much.

The sofa dipped as Tom dropped down beside him.

"Sorry," Tom apologised as they bumped shoulders, but he didn't move away.

He kept his eyes closed. He could feel Tom's shoulder pressing against his. When he inhaled, he could smell the musky scent of Tom's aftershave.

"I'm glad you could come tonight," Tom said after a long pause.

He opened his eyes and stared straight ahead. He was too scared to look in Tom's direction for fear of revealing his true feelings. "Thanks for inviting me," he replied, and took another, much smaller, sip of his drink. This time, it went down without a hiccup.

Tom rested his head back on the sofa, beside his own. "You're off to uni in a few weeks, right?"

"Yeah, to Dunedin."

"To do what?"

"Law," he sighed. Suddenly, the thought of leaving Wellington had lost its appeal.

"You don't seem too happy about it," Tom replied. He must have picked up on the distinct lack of enthusiasm in Sam'v voice.

Sam was about to reply when Tom sprang to his feet and walked over to the bookcase. He took a record down from the top shelf, carefully removed the delicate vinyl disc inside, and placed it on the turntable. "I saw these guys in Auckland last year. They were pretty awesome," he said, lowering the needle carefully into place.

There was a crackle, followed by a second or two of silence, and then the room was filled with music. Tom turned the volume up.

Tom held his gaze for a second. He really did have the bluest eyes Sam had ever seen. They were like two sapphires speckled with gold.

"You know this song?" Tom asked.

"Yeah, of course," he replied, and lowered his eyes.

A cold gust of wind blew in through the open window. It sent the curtains ballooning into the room and rattled the bathroom door at the end of the hall. He tried to disguise a shiver, but Tom noticed.

"Cold, eh?"

"Yeah, a bit."

"Lean forward, then." Tom reached behind him for the merino blanket that was draped over the back of the sofa. His face came to within centimetres of Tom's chest. He could feel the heat radiating from Tom's body.

Tom sat back down and spread the blanket over both their legs. "Better?"

"Yes, thanks."

He was smiling like a buffoon but he couldn't help it. Thankfully, Tom had his eyes closed.

He laid his head back and took a deep breath.

Before the end of the next track, they were both fast asleep.

chapter six

IT TOOK SAM a moment to remember exactly where he was. Sunshine was streaming in through a gap in the curtains, straight into his eyes, and he had to squint against the glare. Slowly, he raised his head and looked around the room.

Tom was still sitting beside him, dead to the world, his neck twisted at an unnatural angle; no doubt, he would have a sore neck later. For a second, he contemplated waking him up, but then he decided against it. What would he say to him if he did?

As soon as he moved, the contents of his stomach sloshed against the sides and he retched. Clutching a hand to his mouth, he forced himself to swallow. The acidic vomit burnt his throat on the way back down. With a shudder of disgust, he wiped the cold sweat from his forehead and clambered to his feet. Tom made a groaning sound and shifted position, but he didn't wake.

He kept one eye on the sofa as he retrieved his coat and shoes from the corner of the room and crept barefoot towards the door.

Before he had taken half a dozen steps, another wave of nausea washed over him and he had to stop. He closed his eyes, bit down on his bottom lip, and waited for the feeling to pass.

The air outside was fresh and clean compared with the closeness of the apartment. He took a deep breath and waited for his head to clear sufficiently to descend the steps safely. The wooden treads felt wet and slimy underfoot, and he gripped the banisters for support. The path at the bottom was covered with gravel, and it hurt the soles of his feet.

His right shoe slipped on with ease, but the back of his left shoe got wedged beneath the heel. "For fuck's sake," he cursed, bending down and freeing it with his finger.

Two girls were waiting at the bus stop opposite. One of the girls whispered something into the other's ear. They both giggled and glanced in his direction. He couldn't hear what they were saying, but he was clearly the butt of their joke. He looked away and hoped that neither of them knew his sister.

Instead of heading for home, he made for the beach, taking the backstreets just in case he ran into anybody he knew. It was almost seven o'clock now, and his mother usually walked Patch early on a Sunday.

When he reached the bay, he climbed over the low wall that separated the beach from the road and sat down on the damp sand. His head was still swimming, and although he could feel the water seeping through his pants, he made no effort to move.

Looking south across the bay, he had a perfect view of planes coming in to land at Wellington airport. The wind was gusting from the northwest, and as the next aircraft started its final approach over Cook Strait, its wings seesawed violently in the crosswind. He felt sorry for the passengers, who were probably feeling just as nauseous as he did right now.

He wrapped his arms round his shins and rested his forehead on his knees. Eyes closed, he concentrated as hard as he could on not being sick—not in public—but within minutes his stomach went into spasm. He staggered to his feet and walked down to the water's edge, away from the puddle of sick. The seagulls that had been circling overhead swooped down and pecked furiously at the sand where he had just been sitting.

"Ugh," he groaned, and turned away in disgust.

It FELT AS if he had only just closed his eyes when the doorbell rang. Still half asleep, he pulled the pillow over his head and rolled onto his side. The last thing he felt like doing was engaging with the world.

A minute passed before the doorbell rang again. Only this time, it was followed by the sound of footsteps in the hall.

"Sam, it's for you!" his sister shouted at the top of her lungs, and then, more quietly, "Go on through," to whomever was at the door.

He glanced at his watch and was surprised to see it was lunchtime already.

"You look like shit," Holly said, appearing in the doorway. She was holding a brown paper bag again. "Jet plane?"

There was a globule of red gelatine between her two front teeth, but he didn't say anything.

"No, thanks," he answered. "What are you doing here?"

She popped another lolly into her mouth and, without waiting to be invited in, walked over to the bed and sat down. She leaned back on her elbows. "So did you want to go see that movie today?"

The way her eyes kept flicking back to his bare chest made him feel more than a little uncomfortable, and he pulled the duvet up under his chin. "Nah, I've got to work this arvo."

She finished off the last of the sweets and tossed the scrunched up paper bag across the room, straight into the waste paper basket. The decision to make her captain of the school netball team had clearly been a good one.

"You sick?" she asked. She let her head hang back on her shoulders. With every intake of breath, her breasts seemed to increase in size.

"No," he replied, his brow furrowing.

"You have mean-as bags under your eyes."

"I went to a party last night," he said, and instantly regretted it.

She sat up and glared at him. "You went to a party and you didn't tell me."

She looked genuinely hurt, and he felt a twinge of guilt. "It was a last-minute decision," he tried to explain, "and anyway, you wouldn't have known anyone there."

She pouted and reclined on her elbows again.

It didn't look as if Holly was planning on leaving any time soon. If he wanted to be rid of her, clearly he would need to be more forceful.

For a moment, he contemplated biting the bullet. *Get*

it over with and lose your virginity, why don't you? Holly was offering it to him on a plate. This really was an opportunity most guys his age would kill for. But instead of feeling grateful, excited, turned on, he felt sick to the pit of his stomach. He shook his head to dislodge the idea.

"Sam, are you home?"

The sound of his mother's voice made him jump. He hadn't heard her arrive home, and before he was able to respond, she was standing in the doorway of his room. Her eyes went straight to Holly, where they stayed.

"Hi, Mrs Wilson," Holly said. She smiled, but the gesture wasn't returned.

"I think you should leave, young lady," his mother said instead.

Holly glanced at him. She had a look of confusion on her face, as if his mother had just told her a joke that she didn't understand.

He threw back the covers and climbed out of bed. He was wearing a pair of tracksuit pants, but in that moment neither his mother nor Holly would have noticed if he had been standing there completely naked. He positioned himself between them. "We weren't doing anything, Mum."

His mother continued as if he wasn't even there.

"I don't know what you thought you were playing at," she hissed. Her voice was ice cold. "But I won't have you exposing my children to that kind of filth, do you hear?"

The room seemed to fade in and out of focus. He took a step backwards and sank down onto the chair next to his desk. It was game over.

He leaned forward on his knees and buried his face in his hands. Out of the corner of his eye, he saw his mother turn on her heels and leave the room. But she was back within seconds, the offending magazine clutched in her right hand. She waved it a couple of times—he was unable to hear what she said over the pounding in his ears—and then threw it down on the mattress next to Holly.

For a long while, he stayed exactly where he was; had he wanted to move, his legs probably wouldn't have cooperated. It was a good ten minutes before they stopped shaking. When he did finally summon up the courage to leave his room, he found his mother sitting at the kitchen table, alone, his great-grandmother's silver cutlery set laid out in front of her.

"I'm sorry I doubted you," she said, holding an Edwardian fish knife up to the light to check for smudges before returning it to the velvet-lined case that was open on the chair next to her. She dipped the corner of a grimy cloth into the cutting solution and set to work on a soup spoon. "I'm sorry I thought you might have been one of them." She exhaled on the back of the spoon and rubbed some more. "I should have known better."

"What did Holly say?" he asked. He knew he would have to tread carefully. The cutlery came out only in a crisis.

She put down the spoon and, sighing deeply, looked him in the eye. "She admitted everything."

"Everything?"

"Yes, everything," she repeated. "I should—"

He was out the door before she had finished the sentence. She called after him—something about his not needing those types of people in his life—but he didn't stop to listen.

He ran most of the way to Holly's house, and by the time he turned into her street, he was gasping for breath. Wheezing, he wiped the sweat from his face with the hem of his T-shirt and climbed the steps to the front door. The sun was almost directly overhead. He could feel its prickly touch on the back of his neck.

Holly lived with her mother and only brother in a large house that had a view of the sailing boats moored in the marina at Evans Bay. Her father lived someplace else. She had told him where, but he didn't remember.

"Sam, how lovely to see you." Holly's mother beamed as she opened the front door. She stood to one side to let him in. "You're right on time. I've just made a tray of ginger crunch."

Clearly, she had no idea what had just happened to her daughter. Any relief he felt was instantaneously subsumed by guilt and shame.

The cream carpet in the hall looked as if it had never been stepped on, so he removed his sneakers and left them on the doorstep.

"Are you looking forward to varsity, Sam?" Holly's mother asked.

"Yes, thanks," he replied. He could barely look her in the eye.

"Holly is in her room. Go on through, and I'll bring you both something to eat."

The last thing he felt like doing was eating, especially something as sickly sweet as ginger crunch, but he smiled and said, "Thanks."

The door to Holly's room was ajar but he knocked anyway.

She was sitting on the bed, her back to the headboard and her knees pulled up under her chin. Although she wasn't crying, it was obvious that she had been, and recently.

He picked nervously at the skin beneath his nails and stared at the sheepskin rug on the floor. Everything he had rehearsed on the way over had gone straight out of his head as he stepped into the room. "I'm so, so sorry," he mumbled after a long, awkward pause.

Holly didn't respond.

"I shouldn't have lied," he continued, "but you know what my mum is like."

The deathly silence was broken only by the clatter of dishes in the hall. A few seconds later, Holly's mother backed into the room. She was carrying a tray of iced tea and ginger crunch, which she set down on the end of the bed. "Here you go, kids. Enjoy."

He looked up to find that Holly was glaring at him. Her lips were pressed together so tight that they had almost disappeared completely.

"Thanks to you, your mum thinks I'm some sort of sexual deviant," she hissed once her own mother had left the room, her voice barely above a whisper.

Instinctively, he looked over his shoulder to check that nobody had heard.

"So are you or aren't you?" she continued, getting straight down to business. And to his horror, she reached under the pillow and withdrew the accursed magazine. She flung it at his feet. "So?"

92

He closed his eyes and willed the ground beneath his feet to open up and swallow him whole, but when he opened his eyes a few seconds later the magazine was still there, the two naked men on the cover grinning up at him. They seemed to be finding his humiliation quite entertaining.

There was no longer any use in denying what was, quite literally, staring him in the face, but still he couldn't bring himself to actually say the words. Instead, he mumbled, "Thanks for not saying anything. I owe you one."

"I'd say," Holly laughed. Her face softened.

Dealing with Holly's anger was one thing; accepting her pity was more than he could bear right now. He didn't want to cry, but he couldn't hold back the tears any longer.

"Are you crying?"

His cheeks were already glowing.

Holly got up off the bed and walked over to where he was standing. Gently she pulled his hands away from his face and lifted his chin. "We're friends, right?" Her eyebrows went up: she was waiting for an answer.

He sniffed and nodded his head.

With one swift kick, she booted the magazine under the bed. "There you go."

He wiped his eyes with the tissue she handed him and smiled.

"To tell you the truth, I'm relieved. I mean, I was beginning to think there was something seriously wrong with me."

A laugh escaped his lips.

"But I'm still pissed that you didn't tell me you're gay!"

"Ahem."

They both spun round to find Holly's mother standing in the doorway. This time, she was holding a plate of Anzac biscuits. She put the plate down on the desk, just inside the door, and backed away without saying a word.

For the second time in as many minutes, he felt as if he couldn't breathe. "I'm sorry. I can't do this."

He had reached the traffic lights at the bottom of Wellington Road before Holly caught up with him. Her jandals slip-slapped against the asphalt as she half-walked, half-ran. "Not so fast, eh," she panted, coming to a stop by his side.

"Sorry," he started to say, but she waved the apology away.

"Don't stress about it. Mum's pretty open-minded. I'll sort her out later." She reached past him and pushed the button on the pedestrian crossing. They waited for the green man in silence.

When they reached Bay Road, Holly ducked into the dairy on the corner. He waited outside, under the shade of the awning. In the distance, he could hear the whirr of the planes at the airport. A small turbo prop seemed to shoot out of the rooftops opposite. He watched as it climbed slowly over the harbour and banked right, towards the south. There wasn't a cloud in the sky, and the atmosphere hung thick and lifeless.

A bead of sweat broke free of his shoulder blades and ran down the length of his spine, between his buttocks.

What the hell is she doing in there? he thought. Five minutes had passed and still Holly hadn't emerged. *How long does it take to buy a couple of ice blocks?*

With the glare of the sun at his back, it was impossible to see into the gloomy interior of the dairy. He took a step towards the door. And promptly collided with somebody coming, head down, in the opposite direction.

"Sorry," he apologised, by reflex more than out of sincerity. He moved aside to let whomever it was pass. Only then did he realise that that somebody was Tom.

"Hi, Sam," Tom said.

For the first time, he noticed the way that Tom's cheeks dimpled when he smiled. All he could manage in reply, though, was, "Hey."

"How were you feeling this morning?" Tom asked.

"Not bad," he lied. "You?"

"Ask me again in ten minutes." Tom waggled the energy drink that he had just purchased. "I'm off to meet the guys for a game of touch and thought I could do with a little help."

For the rest of his life, he would cringe whenever he thought back on what happened next.

Just as he opened his mouth to speak, Holly came bounding out of the dairy, shrieking with laughter.

"I got you a Golden Gaytime!" she roared, "I couldn't help—"

Perhaps it was the mortified expression on his face that cut her off at the pass, or maybe it was the sight of an attractive guy in shorts and a sleeveless T-shirt that did it. Whatever it was, she stopped giggling instantly. She pulled a face and mouthed, "Sorry."

"Hi, I'm Tom." Tom turned and held out his hand.

"Holly," she mumbled.

Tom turned back to face him. "I guess I'd better be going."

He could see Holly out of the corner of his eye. She was staring unashamedly at Tom, her eyes as wide as saucers. Blood was already flooding into his cheeks, but he tried to ignore it.

"See you round, eh?" Tom said as he turned to leave. "Nice to meet you, Holly."

Tom took several steps and then stopped. "Oh," he said, turning round. He looked nervous. "Me and the boys were thinking of heading into town for a few drinks tonight." He paused. "If you fancy it?"

Before he could get a word out, Holly had replied on his behalf. "We'll be there."

Tom nodded and smiled. "I'll text you later, then."

"Fuck, he's hot," Holly squealed as soon as Tom had crossed the road and was out of earshot. "Come on," she said, tugging at his arm, "let's get home. We've got a night out to get ready for!"

IT WAS CLOSE to ten by the time they reached the bus stop.

"Earthquake weather, eh?" Holly said, rubbing at the goose bumps on her arms. He grunted in reply. His insides had been twisted in knots all day, and he still felt too nauseous to speak.

Evans Bay was as calm as a millpond and the water shone like polished silver in the moonlight. She was right; the stillness was eerie. He peered down the road again. There was still no sign of the bus.

Despite the cold, his palms felt warm and clammy. "I told you to bring a coat," he growled when Holly shivered for the third or fourth time in as many minutes. Why did nobody ever listen to him?

"Sorry, Dad!" she snapped back. "I told you: I don't want to be carrying a jacket all night. Anyway, once I get a few drinks inside me, I'll be a box of fluffies."

He glanced down at his wrist again, and then remembered that he had forgotten to put his watch back on after his shower. He shoved his hands into the pockets of his jeans and leaned back on his heels. *There's nothing to be worried about,* he tried to convince himself. He took a deep breath and closed his eyes. *You're just going for a drink. That's all.*

He heard the bus before he saw it—that familiar sound of electricity poles passing over junctions in the network of cables overhead. Slowly, the bus rounded the corner and came into view. The yellow glare of its headlights obscured the driver completely. He walked over to the edge of the footpath and held out his left hand. The bus crawled to a stop several metres further down the road.

A few minutes later, they turned into Waitoa Road and began the short climb up to the bus tunnel, which linked the eastern suburbs of Wellington with the city centre. During the day it was possible to see sunlight at the other end, but at night the oval entrance was no more than a black smudge on the side of the hill.

He hated confined spaces. Once when they were children, his sister had locked him in the wooden chest at the foot of their parents' bed during a game of hide and seek. He had had nightmares about it for months after.

He closed his eyes and tried to picture the wide open expanse of Lyall Bay, the waves lapping peacefully on the shore, but the image, so carefully constructed, vanished the instant the bus driver slammed his foot on the brake.

The bus came to a screeching, jarring halt, and the half a dozen passengers who were standing in the aisle shot forward and almost ended up in a heap on the floor. "Watch it, mate!" a voice yelled from somewhere behind him.

The driver paid no attention. Instead, he reached up for the walkie-talkie above his head and grunted into the mouthpiece, "Two guys in the tunnel. Over."

Sam plucked a tissue from his pocket and wiped the perspiration from his forehead. The driver's rapping on the steering wheel was only making his anxiety worse, and when Holly saw that his hands were shaking, she gave him a concerned look. "You OK?"

He nodded.

Breathe. Just breathe.

An eternity seemed to pass before the radio crackled back into life: "Proceed with caution. The police have been notified. Over."

And with a lurch that threw him and the other passengers forward in their seats again, they crawled forwards, out into the still night air.

He was out of his seat before the bus had turned into Courtenay Place. Elbowing his way through the crowd, he jumped down onto the footpath, sucking in a lungful of fresh air.

"Are you sure you're OK?" Holly asked, appearing beside him. She was rummaging in her bag and pulled out a packet of bubble-gum. "Want one?"

He shook his head. "Come on—they'll be waiting."

But when they reached the spot where Tom had arranged to meet them, he was nowhere to be seen.

The taxi rank on the corner of Courtenay Place and Tory Street was full, the drivers standing between their vehicles, smoking and chatting while they waited for their next fare. "Need a ride?" one of the drivers called out, spotting them loitering on the footpath nearby. He shook his head and turned away.

"Are you sure this is the right place?" Holly asked. She blew a pink bubble with her gum. It reached the size of a large orange before it burst. She flicked the gum back into her mouth with her tongue and resumed chewing.

He nodded, craning his neck to see further down the street. From force of habit, he reached into his jacket pocket for his cigarettes. The packet was unopened, and he ripped off the cellophane cover. He inhaled deeply and the end glowed incandescent, the muscles in his shoulders relaxing before the nicotine had begun to leach into his bloodstream.

"Are you sure?" Holly asked again.

"Yes," he exhaled. "They must be running late."

"I can't see them anywhere. Can't we just go in out of the cold? I can't feel my nipples any more."

"Here, take my coat." He removed his jacket and handed it to her. It was several sizes too big and it hung from her shoulders like a sack.

He held the cigarette between his thumb and index

finger, the burning end sheltered in the palm of his hand. He stared at it intently, as if it might offer some kind of clue as to what they should do next. He was still lost in thought when Tom and Jarryd came tearing round the corner.

"Sorry we're late," Tom panted. "Have you been waiting long?"

He shook his head.

"We just arrived, actually," Holly said.

"This bright spark nearly got us arrested just now," Tom said, motioning to Jarryd, who was gasping for breath. They looked as if they had been running for their lives.

"What do you mean?" he asked.

Tom must have seen the concerned look on his face, because he continued, "Don't worry. It's all good. We got caught running through the bus tunnel, but we managed to leg it before the police arrived." Tom punched Jarryd playfully on the arm. "I told you we should've got the bus, toss. Sam, you remember Jarryd, eh?"

He had been only half-listening and blurted out the first thing to come into his head. "The crusher?"

Jarryd roared with laughter and clasped him round the shoulders. Sam had his hands in his pockets and almost lost his balance. "This one's a keeper," Jarryd boomed. But Tom wasn't listening.

"I doubt you'll get in wearing those," Tom said, nodding at his feet. Sam's heart sank.

He had been so preoccupied with getting there on time that he hadn't given his sneakers a second thought. Of course, most of the bars in the city would insist on leather shoes on a Saturday night.

Tom didn't seem overly concerned, though. "Wait over there."

There was no time for questions. Tom turned and, without saying another word, walked past the doorman, into the bar. Jarryd grinned, shrugged his shoulders, and followed hot on his heels.

He stood where he was for a moment, not quite sure what to do next. Whatever Tom was up to, he doubted it was strictly above board. The last thing he needed was to get into trouble just before he was due to leave for university. His mother would kill him.

Holly tugged on his sleeve. "Come on. We'd better do as he says." She put an arm through his and dragged him over to the window Tom had pointed to.

The footpath was teeming with people. Two young girls tottered past. They didn't look much older than his sister and were holding on to each other for support.

"IDs, please," he heard the doorman say. One of the girls giggled nervously and flicked her hair back, but the doorman didn't bat an eyelid. "Sorry, girls. You're not coming in without ID."

He breathed a sigh of relief. At least he had had the good sense to bring his driver's licence with him.

When Tom rapped on the window behind him, he almost jumped out of his skin. He spun round, his heart in his throat. Tom pointed to his right, towards the entrance to the bar, and mouthed something that he didn't understand. "What?" He shrugged his shoulders.

Tom rolled his eyes and repeated himself, but it was no use; the music was too loud. The whole window was vibrating like a giant speaker. Tom glanced over his shoulder and then slid the window open a few centimetres. "Is he watching?"

The doorman. Of course.

He glanced to his left. Thankfully, a bachelorette party had just arrived. He shook his head. In the next instant, Tom thrust a pair of shoes through the gap. "Quick, give me yours."

Holly stepped forward and took the shoes. She tucked them inside her jacket, out of sight. He hoped to God the doorman wasn't watching, but he didn't dare stop to check.

"You're OK. He's not looking this way," Holly said, as if she had read his mind. He slipped out of his sneakers and handed them up to Tom, who then vanished into the crowd.

"Quickly, put them on," Holly whispered under her breath. She pressed the shoes into his hands.

"They fit?"

He wriggled his toes. The leather was still warm. "Yes," he replied absently.

"Come on then," she said, pulling him towards the entrance. "It's freezing out here, and I need a drink."

He slipped the driver's licence from his wallet, ready for inspection, but the doorman gave it only a cursory glance and waved them both through.

Inside, it looked as if the entire population of Wellington was trying to squeeze within the same four walls. The air was thick with cigarette smoke and each breath clawed in his throat. If it hadn't been for Tom, he would have walked straight back out the door.

Holly put a hand on his shoulder and leaned in close to his ear. "Do you see him?" she shouted over the music.

He gazed out over the sea of heads, but there was no sign of Tom. Red and green strobe lighting flashed overhead, illuminating faces at random. The rhythmic thud of the bass resonated through his chest like a second heartbeat. He sank back down on his heels and shook his head; it was like looking for a needle in a haystack.

"Come on." Holly grabbed him by the wrist and pulled him into the crowd. Only when they reached the bar did she let go of his arm. "Wait here," she shouted over her shoulder and slipped through a gap in the wall of bodies. From a distance of several metres, he watched as she stepped up onto the brass footrest beneath the bar and leaned across the counter. She was wearing a low-cut top that showed off her breasts, and within minutes, she was back, a drink in both hands and a triumphant look on her face.

They sipped their drinks in silence. The music was much too loud for conversation, and Tom was still nowhere to be seen.

When he saw Sutcliffe in the crowd, he almost vomited on the spot. His ribs were still sore, and the bruise under his eye, although no longer dark purple, was still a mottled yellow colour. Instinctively, he raised one arm to protect his middle. *Oh God*, he thought, *not again.* It was one thing to be shamed in front of a few ageing council workers; it was something else entirely to be humiliated in front of Tom.

"What's the matter?" Holly asked. She must have seen the blood drain from his face. She lowered her glass and glanced over her shoulder. Right on cue, Sutcliffe turned and looked in their direction. It took a few seconds for Sutcliffe's brain to catch up with his eyes. Slowly, a malevolent grin spread across his face.

"Far!" Sutcliffe exclaimed and sauntered over to where he and Holly were standing. "Fancy seeing you two here, eh?" Sutcliffe plucked the drink from his hand and laughed. "You shouldn't have."

He was too stunned to put up a fight. For Sutcliffe, it was easier than taking candy from a baby. But Holly was less easily intimidated.

"Do one," she said, snatching back the drink just as Sutcliffe was about to take a swig. Beer sloshed from the neck of the bottle, down the front of Sutcliffe's shirt.

"Far," Sutcliffe cried and shook his head. "Getting the girls to look after you now, eh, Sam?"

The collar on his shirt suddenly felt several sizes too small. He ran a hand through his hair and almost whispered, "Please just leave us alone."

Sutcliffe opened his mouth and, to his surprise, closed it again without saying a word.

"Hey, we've been looking for you everywhere," Tom said, appearing at his side as if by magic. Tom's eyes didn't leave Sutcliffe as he leaned in and asked, "Is this a friend of yours?"

A shiver went down his spine as Tom's breath brushed the side of neck, just behind his left ear. He shook his head.

With a flick of the chin, Tom summoned Jarryd, Wiremu and several others guys, whom he recognised vaguely from the party at Tom's flat. They clustered in a group directly behind Sutcliffe, who seemed to shrink in size before his very eyes. Sutcliffe wasn't known to shy away from a scrap when the odds were stacked in his favour, but this time, he was clearly outmatched. Jarryd crossed his arms over his chest, his muscles bulging beneath the tattoos that decorated his skin from shoulder to wrist.

Sutcliffe slunk off without saying a word.

"Here, I got you these," Tom said. He was holding two bottles in his right hand. He gave one to Holly and handed him the other.

"Thanks," he said. He pressed his lips together into a half smile, but inside, he was still praying for the ground to open up and swallow him. He had never been so humiliated in his life. It was a while before his pulse returned to normal.

The bar was nearing capacity now, yet the stream of bodies filing in through the door showed no sign of letting up.

"Follow me," Tom said, leaning in so that their faces were only centimetres apart. His breath was warm and smelled of hops. Not wanting to be left alone—Holly had spotted a group of girls from her netball team and had gone to say hello—he followed Tom out onto the terrace, where the music wasn't quite so deafening.

"He'd better let me off the fuckin' bench this year," a small, wiry guy called Franklin was complaining to the guy sitting next to him. "I hardly got any fuckin' game time last season. I tell you, I'm this close to telling him to get fucked." He held his thumb and index finger a centimetre apart. "This fuckin' close!" he hissed and sculled the last of his beer. Franklin slammed the glass down on the table so hard that he was surprised it didn't shatter.

"Try kicking the ball between the posts and he might let you," Tom replied. Franklin glared back at him, and for a moment, he thought there might be a fight. But then Franklin's face cracked into a large grin and he laughed.

"How do you know Tom?" Jarryd asked, appearing at his side when Tom went to the bar to buy another round of drinks.

"He works with my dad," he replied.

"You're John's son?"

He nodded. He hooked his thumbs under his belt and leaned back on his heels. "How long have you known Tom?" It was his turn to speak and he couldn't think of anything else to say.

"I can't remember, bro." Jarryd shrugged his shoulders. "We've been mates since for ever." Jarryd's mouth twitched upwards at the sides as though he had just remembered something funny.

"Are you a builder, too?"

Jarryd shook his head. "Nah—a mechanic. And as for those two clowns," he pointed his empty glass at the others, "Franklin's a sparky and Jensen does something with computers." Franklin and Jensen both looked up at the mention of their names. "Tom tells me you're off to uni."

Thankfully, Tom reappeared before he had to answer any more questions.

"Thanks," he said accepting what appeared to be a whisky and Coke. "The next ones are one me, though."

When Tom smiled, he felt his whole body respond.

Tom was wearing a fitted shirt, the cuffs folded back past his elbows, and the hairs on his forearms shone like gold thread beneath the glow of the heat lamps.

"Are you OK—you know?" Tom asked.

He took a sip of his drink and nodded. Never in his life had he had such an overwhelming urge to kiss another person. Tom's lips looked like silk and he wondered whether they would feel as soft.

His daydreaming was interrupted by the appearance of a girl he didn't know. But clearly, she knew Tom, and he felt a pang of nausea in his gut as Tom leaned in and kissed her on the cheek. She rested one hand on Tom's arm and reached up to whisper something into his ear. He noticed, with a growing resentment, that she allowed her hand to linger for a moment after she had finished speaking.

"This is Sam," Tom turned and gestured to him with his glass. "Sam, this is Zoe."

He forced himself to smile.

Zoe glanced in his direction, but she seemed to look straight through him. She shifted her attention straight back to Tom.

The sense of euphoria that he had felt just minutes earlier was already turning to despair. Although he didn't have a clue who she was, or what she meant to Tom, it was crystal clear that she had no intention of leaving any time soon. Short of removing her physically, he was stuck with her.

He looked over to where Holly had been standing when he had last seen her, but there was no sign of her now. For a moment, he contemplated going in search of her but quickly weighed it up against the probability of bumping into Sutcliffe and decided that he would stay put. *Better the devil you know,* he reasoned.

"I don't know how he does it," Jarryd said, appearing at his side. He gave Jarryd a blank look.

"Girls," Jarryd explained loudly. He pointed his glass at Tom. "They buzz round him like flies round shit."

Tom looked up and gave them a mischievous grin. Jarryd was right; there was something magnetic about him. His whole face lit up when he smiled. Tom winked and then turned his attention back to Zoe.

Sam was standing too far away to be able to hear exactly what Tom was saying, but Zoe's body language suddenly changed. She squared her shoulders as if she had just been told bad news. When she walked away, he tried not to smile.

"What was that about flies and shit?" Tom asked, sneaking up on Jarryd.

Jarryd took a step backward, but he wasn't fast enough. Tom's arm shot round his neck and pulled him down to waist level, in a headlock. "What was that you said?"

"She given you the flick already?" Jarryd goaded, trying in vain to prise himself free. Most of his drink ended up on the floor in the process. But instead of letting go, Tom tightened his grip and Jarryd made a horrible choking sound.

Jarryd drew his fist back to hit Tom but instead knocked a full glass of red wine out of the hand of a girl standing behind him. The glass flew into the air, drenching those underneath, and smashed into a thousand pieces on the polished concrete floor. The screams promptly attracted the attention of the doorman, who started towards them, his face like thunder.

"Let's get out of here." Tom grabbed him by the arm and pulled him into the crowd.

He felt guilty leaving without Holly, but there was no time to look for her now. Still, he hesitated for a moment when they reached the fire exit at the rear of the bar.

"Come on," Tom said. He turned and followed him through the door, out into the fresh air.

"Where are we going?"

They were walking away from Courtenay Place, towards the waterfront, and he had to increase his pace just to keep up. Tom darted between two cars that were parked up at the side of the street and crossed over to the other side.

"You'll see."

Tom's shoes were a size too small, and by the time they reached the north end of Lambton Quay, they had rubbed large blisters on his heels. He was about to ask whether they would be walking much further when Tom stopped and announced, "We're here."

They were standing outside a large stone building. The ground floor was hidden behind a three-metre-high wooden fence and attached to the padlocked gate was a sign that read *Danger, Keep Out* in large red lettering.

He looked around, confused.

Tom produced a key from his pocket and inserted it into the lock, which sprang open with a snap.

Sam took a step back and glanced around. Was Tom trying to get them both arrested? He opened his

SAM

mouth to protest, but Tom had already disappeared.

"Come on!" a disembodied voice called out. He took a deep breath and, checking again that nobody was watching, followed Tom into the darkness.

It was pitch-black inside the building and it took a couple of minutes for his eyes to fully adjust to the lack of light. Slowly, the foyer of an apartment block materialised.

"What the hell are we doing?" he asked. Tom was sitting on the third step of a concrete staircase.

"Don't stress—we're perfectly safe. Just watch your head and follow me." Tom jumped to his feet and headed on up the steps. At the top of the first flight, he stopped and yelled down to him, "It'll be worth it. Trust me."

His thighs were burning by the third floor, and at the tenth, he had to ask Tom to pause for a moment while he caught his breath. He was wheezing like an asthmatic by the time they reached the top.

"Nearly there," Tom said. His voice echoed off the bare breezeblock walls. They were standing in a large, cavernous space that would soon be divided neatly into individual units. Tom motioned towards a metal door in the corner.

The moon had risen while they were in the bar. Its light traced a silver path across the blackness of the water, cleaving the harbour in two. On the far side of the water, the lights of the Petone foreshore twinkled like stars fallen to Earth. Tom was right; the view from the roof was truly breathtaking.

Tom walked across the tarsealed roof and sat on the stone ledge. Casually, as if the street were only a few metres below, he swung his legs out over the edge and let them hang in the air.

Sam gasped and instinctively took a step backwards. He pressed his sweat-soaked back against the door, which had clicked shut behind him.

"Come and have a seat," Tom shouted over his shoulder. "It's perfectly safe. I built it myself."

It was too late now to tell Tom that he had a pathological fear of heights. Mustering every ounce of courage, he took a couple of steps forward—slowly, as if the floor were made of thin ice that might crack at any moment. He made it halfway before he had to stop. He couldn't go any further.

"What do you think?" Tom turned and smiled. "Pretty cool, eh?" He nodded in agreement.

Tom arched his eyebrows. "You don't look very relaxed." He hopped down off the wall and walked back towards him. "You don't like heights?"

He gulped and shook his head.

"Sorry, I didn't think." Tom sat down at his feet and patted the floor beside him. "We can stay here."

It was a relief to feel the floor solid beneath him. He reached into his pocket for his cigarettes. There was only one left. He offered it to Tom, who shook his head.

"Here." Tom held out a silver hipflask. "It will make you feel better."

He took a large gulp.

His whole body seemed to convulse, but somewhere inside, a flame ignited. "What the hell is that?" he coughed, shaking his head. His eyes filled with tears.

"Bourbon."

He coughed again and dried his eyes on the neck of his sweater. Far away, a siren wailed. Police, fire, ambulance—it was anybody's guess.

"Did you play in the final last year?" he asked after they had been sitting in silence for a while. Tom was lying on the floor, gazing up at the stars.

"Yeah."

He took another, smaller sip from the flask. "I heard you played well."

"We lost. Thirty-nil."

"Oh," he replied, and gave himself a mental kick in the shin.

The subject of girls was always going to come up—it always did sooner or later—but he still felt an intense disappointment when Tom asked, "What's the deal with you and Holly?"

He didn't answer immediately. He took a deep breath and shifted in his seat. "What do you mean?" he asked, stalling for time. He knew full well what Tom meant.

"You know she likes you, don't you?"

He swallowed. His throat was bone dry. He removed the cap from the hipflask and took another sip. "Yeah, I know." He needed to shift the spotlight off of himself, and quickly, before Tom had a chance to ask any more questions. "And you—are you seeing anyone?"

Tom sat upright. He cupped his hands around the back of his head and stared out across the harbour. "No, not at the moment. So you're not interested in Holly, then?" Tom batted the ball straight back into his court.

"No, you dumb shit," was what he really wanted to say. "Can't you see it's you I want?" But, instead, he settled for a hackneyed, "We're just good friends."

It was freezing cold on the roof, and despite the warming effects of the whisky, he began to shiver. Tom noticed straight away.

"You're cold." Tom took his coat off. Ignoring his protests, Tom draped it around his shoulders. "Here—I don't need it."

He could see the hairs on Tom's forearms. They were standing on end. But he didn't say anything. The jacket was warm, and with each intake of breath, he caught the faint aroma of aftershave.

Tom leaned back on his hands and looked up at the sky. "Have you ever been to Lake Tekapo?"

He looked at Tom and gave him a questioning look.

"I spent a night there a couple of years back," Tom explained. "I was on my way down to Queenstown to see some mates who were working the ski season. There's isn't much there—in Tekapo. Just a motel and a few shops, really. But at night, when the stars come out, it's something else. You have to see it."

He looked up into the darkness above them. The light from the streetlamps below obscured most of the night sky, but out over the pitch-black waters of Cook Strait it was possible to see a smattering of stars.

"I'll take you sometime if you want."

He turned his head towards Tom, only to find that Tom was watching him. Instead of looking away, Tom held his gaze, his eyes shining like sapphires. Tom smiled and a surge of electricity coursed through his body.

There was a long awkward silence before Tom spoke again.

"Come on," Tom said, getting to his feet. His voice had changed. He sounded almost annoyed now. "Let's go, eh."

chapter seven

"SAM, WILL YOU please just tell me what's wrong?"

His mother put down her knife and fork and turned towards him. "I know that something is bothering you. You've been moping around the house for days now."

The tone of her voice roused him from his daydream. "Sorry?"

"Is something the matter? You've hardly eaten a thing." She nodded at his plate. He looked down at his dinner, as if seeing it for the first time.

"Leave the boy alone," his father intervened on his behalf. He had a mouthful of food, and a speck of potato flew across the table.

"I'm fine," he said, "I just feel a bit sick—that's all."

His mother reached over and placed a hand on his forehead. "You don't feel hot, although you do look a little pale. Go and lie down. I'll put your dinner in the oven to keep warm." She took his plate away before he could protest and placed it on the kitchen bench, out of reach. "I'll come and check on you in a bit. Now go."

Obediently, he got to his feet and retreated to the sanctuary of his room. The following morning, he made sure he was up and out long before his parents awoke.

There was still a week to go till Christmas Day but the supermarket car park was already full by the time he arrived at work. Lately, he had been working as many shifts as he could. Each dollar earned now was one less he would need to find in Dunedin.

"Here, put this on." His supervisor thrust a red and green felt hat into his hands. Sewn onto the peak was a silver bell, which jingled with every movement. "Don't worry," she said, seeing the look of horror on his face, "everybody will be wearing one." She handed him his float. "Number eight, please. I'll send someone to relieve you for lunch at one." But by half past one, there was still no sign of his replacement and his stomach was growling angrily in protest.

"Do you have a loyalty card?" he asked the lady he was serving. He glanced at the long line of customers, which now snaked down the aisle opposite. If they didn't relieve him now, it would be at least another quarter of an hour before he could hope to get away.

"Thanks." He swiped the card and handed it back across the counter.

He was so focused on what he was doing that he hadn't noticed Tom waiting patiently in line. When he spotted him, he almost dropped the jar of pickles he was holding.

"You've just scanned that twice."

He could hardly hear the man standing in front of him over the pounding in his ears. "You've scanned that already," the man repeated, accusingly.

"Sorry," he apologised. He felt his face turn beetroot.

He glanced at Tom, who grinned and rolled his eyes.

"Hey, how's it going?" Tom smiled as he stepped up to the counter.

"Good thanks," he replied. He tried to concentrate on the job at hand, picking up the first item, a twelve-pack of beer, and scanning the barcode on the base of the box. "You?"

His face was still burning. He hoped to God it didn't look as red as it felt.

"Yeah, not bad. Just getting a few essentials for Christmas." Tom was wearing a loose, sleeveless T-shirt, which billowed outwards as he lifted the beers back into the empty trolley.

For the briefest of moments, Sam had an unobstructed view of Tom's chest. His nipples stood erect, two pink discs on otherwise unblemished skin. He managed to look away just in time.

"Are you spending the holidays at home with your folks?" Tom asked, straightening up.

Sam picked up the next item, a bag of loose apples, and punched in the corresponding product code. "Yeah, my grandparents will be up from Christchurch on the twenty-fourth," he replied. His heart was pounding dangerously fast.

Right on cue, his lunch reliever appeared. He finished serving Tom and walked with him towards the exit. "Let me give you a hand," he said, reaching into the trolley before Tom could say no.

Tom tucked the carton of beers under one arm and carried the remaining bags in his other hand. "I was hoping that I'd run into you, actually."

"You were?" he blurted out and immediately wanted to kick himself.

Be cool, you dick.

"A few of us are going away over the New Year," Tom continued. "I—we—wondered if you fancied coming along."

"Oh—um," he stammered. He was completely lost for words.

"I mean, it was just an idea," Tom added quickly. "If you don't want to—"

"No," he cut Tom off, "I'd like that." Tom was adorable when he was flustered, and he had to concentrate hard to keep from grinning ear to ear.

"WHAT DO YOU mean, you're going away for New Year?"

His mother glared at him. She was standing at the kitchen sink, arms elbow-deep in soap suds.

"You know we always spend New Year together. It's a family tradition. Your gran and grandad will be here, and they'll be really disappointed if you're not!"

He had been fully prepared for a fight. He knew his mother wouldn't back down quietly. But the one thing he hadn't been expecting was his father to come to his rescue.

"The boy can go if he wants to." His father folded the newspaper he was reading and placed it on the table in front of him. Then he crossed his arms, leaned back in his seat, and addressed him directly. "Where will you be going?"

"The Hawke's Bay, Dad," he answered, trying not to

look at his mother. He could feel her eyes burning a hole in his back.

"And how long will you be gone?"

"Just a few nights."

"I suppose you'll need some money, then?"

He glanced at his mother for help, but she turned away. His father wasn't known for his generosity; quite the opposite, in fact.

His father stood up, walked silently to the coat rack in the hall, and returned a moment later holding a thick wad of bank notes.

"Where did you get all that money from?" his mother shrieked at the sight of the cash.

"My good friends at the TAB," his father replied, a rare smile flashing across his face. He peeled off two crisp fifty-dollar notes and flicked them across the table.

Sam looked down at the twin faces of Sir Apirana Ngata. Should he pocket the cash, or was this some sort of test?

"Don't you want the money?" his father asked, his brow furrowing.

"Um—yes—thanks very much, Dad." Cautiously, he reached for the money, but his father was as good as his word. The clip around the ear that he was expecting never came.

THE MORNING OF the thirtieth, he was up at the crack of dawn, and by the time Tom pulled up outside and honked the car horn, he had changed his clothes completely—twice.

"Sam, will you come here a moment, please."

119

He put down the bag he was carrying and turned towards the kitchen. His mother was sitting at the table, her hands folded neatly in her lap. She motioned to the empty chair beside her. "Sit down a moment, will you."

Tom's car was parked up across the street. He could see Jarryd sitting in the front passenger seat, his left elbow propped on the open window, his fingertips rapping on the roof. Reluctantly, he sat down. Hopefully, whatever his mother was wanting to say wouldn't take long.

"I want you to pray with me."

Her voice was firm, and she began straight away, before he had a chance to protest. She reached forward and took his hands in her own.

"Father, we ask that You protect Sam and that You keep him on the path of righteousness."

He wasn't listening to a word that his mother was saying. *Please, please, don't come looking for me*, he was praying instead. From the doorstep, Tom would have a perfect view into the kitchen.

His mother kept a firm hold on his hands when she finished. He knew exactly what she was waiting for; it was always the same. She gave his fingers a gentle squeeze of encouragement.

"Dear God," he began. It would be quicker and much less painful to do as she wanted.

Tom had to lower the visor and squint over the steering wheel just to see through the glare as they sailed along the urban motorway, out of the city.

There wasn't a cloud in the sky. Clearly, it was going to be another scorcher of a day, and over the hill, in the Wairarapa, it would be even hotter. The farmers had been facing water restrictions for weeks already and their paddocks looked as if they belonged more in the Middle East than in New Zealand.

"Move over, will you," Franklin grumbled at Jensen. "Your fat arse is spilling over onto my seat."

Sam was sitting on Jensen's left, and as Jensen shuffled over, away from Franklin, he was pinned against the door. He glanced down at the blur of tarmac and hoped the lock would hold.

"Now, now, kids." Jarryd turned and peered through the gap between the two front seats. "We've got a long way to go yet."

Jarryd was right; it was well past lunch before they reached the outskirts of Napier. They sailed through the city without stopping and carried on along State Highway 2 for another ten kilometres before turning off the main drag and winding their way through the hills, towards the coast.

The beach at Waipatiki was a half-moon bay nestled between steep cliffs at either end. Aside from a cluster of beach houses and a small camping ground, there wasn't much to write home about. He gazed out the window at their bach. It looked at least fifty years old, and the weatherboard was rotting in several places.

"Here we are. You can stop fighting now." Tom swung the car onto the drive and cut the engine.

Sam opened the car door and groaned unashamedly with pleasure as he stretched out his legs.

"I'll find the key. You guys start unloading the car," Tom said, disappearing around the back of the house, leaving Sam and the others to unpack the mountain of supplies.

The inside of the bach looked just as run down as the outside. The chocolate-brown carpet in the living room was threadbare in places, and none of the armchairs matched. He wandered over to the bookcase in the corner and plucked a dog-eared paperback from the hodgepodge on the shelves. He glanced casually at the cover. A Mills & Boon with a faded cerise cover. He returned it to the pile.

"There's one twin room and two doubles," Tom said, dumping a large box of groceries on the kitchen table. "Deano's girlfriend has already called first dibs on one of the doubles." Tom turned to Jensen and Franklin, who had just wandered through the door. "You guys take the twin, eh?"

"I'm game if you are?" Jensen nudged Franklin in the ribs with his elbow. Franklin grunted in reply and then turned and walked back out to the car.

"You might as well take the other double," Tom said to Sam.

"But what about you—where will you sleep?"

"I'm more than happy outside. You take the bed."

He didn't like to press the point, so he just smiled and said, "Thanks."

As it was, by the time Deano and his girlfriend, Amber, arrived, Tom had assembled his tent on the lawn and everything was settled. It was a warm evening and the sun was still hanging low over the horizon. He felt the knot of tension in his neck and shoulders slowly unravel.

"I saw some insect repellent on the shelf in the kitchen," Tom said, seeing him swat at another mosquito, which was trying to land on his arm. He had already scratched several bites until they bled. He went inside and covered every centimetre of exposed flesh with the most pungent and toxic-smelling spray he could find.

Tom had hardly said a thing to him all day, but now that the beers were flowing he began to chat more freely.

"I'm glad you could come with us," Tom said, plucking another two bottles from the chilly bin beside him. He was sitting on the edge of the deck, his bare feet on the grass below. "Here."

"Thanks," Sam said, accepting the drink. Tom scooched over so he could sit down.

"Have you been here before?" Sam asked.

"Nah, but my sister has. She told us about this place." He looked around, as if seeing the shabby décor for the first time. "Maybe I'll take back that Christmas present I gave her." Tom winked and Sam laughed despite himself.

The next day was New Year's Eve, and they spent most of the day lazing on the beach.

"You're gonna have a mean sunburn tomorrow," Jensen lectured Franklin, who had stubbornly turned down every offer of sunscreen.

Sam slipped his polo shirt over his head and grimaced as the fabric rubbed against his skin. He wriggled his shoulders and brushed the crystallised salt from his arms and legs.

"Is Eve still overseas?" he heard Amber ask Jarryd. She was standing upwind of the group, and as she shook the sand from her beach towel, it blew straight back in their faces.

"Oi, watch out!" Deano yelled, wiping the grit from his eyes.

"Yeah, I think so," Jarryd replied. "At least Tom hasn't said otherwise."

"Is Eve Tom's sister?" he asked Amber when they were walking back to the bach. Tom and Jarryd had gone on ahead to light the barbecue.

Amber laughed. She was holding her beach bag by the strap and was swinging it back and forth like a pendulum. "No, she's his girlfriend."

He didn't hear what she said next; it took all his concentration to put one foot in front of the other. He didn't know why he had assumed Tom was single. It made sense that he wasn't; guys like Tom never were.

By the time they arrived back at the beach house, Tom had already showered and was standing on the lawn, wringing out his wet togs. His towel was tied low around his waist. Sam kept his eyes to the floor and made straight for his room without saying a word.

He was sitting on the bed, trying to read, when Tom appeared in the doorway a quarter of an hour later.

Tom crossed his arms and leaned against the doorframe. He had changed into his jeans and put on a fresh T-shirt. The white cotton made the skin on his forearms look almost brown. "Dinner will be ready soon," said Tom.

He turned down the corner of the page that he was reading and returned the book to the bedside table. As it was, he hadn't been able to concentrate on the book. Each time he started a sentence, his mind wandered straight back to what Amber had said.

"I'll be out in a minute," he said. He tried to sound as upbeat as he could.

It was barely seven o'clock and Jensen was already drunk. What was more, he seemed to be getting louder by the minute. "Take me to the vet, bro," he howled, flexing his biceps, "cos these puppies are sick!"

"You're sick, dick," Franklin answered, and continued eating his corncob.

Sam glanced around for a place to sit and eat. The only free seat was next to Tom. He kept his eyes to the floor as he walked across the deck and sat down.

"When are you off to uni?" Franklin asked, after a few minutes had passed.

"Um—" He swallowed the mouthful he was chewing. "In February." He cleared his throat with a cough. "Term one starts in February," he repeated. He could feel Tom's eyes on him but he pretended not to notice. "I'll probably head down a few days before that, though."

"It's Dunedin you're going to, eh?"

He nodded his head.

"Respect." Franklin raised his bottle in a toast. "I hear it goes off down there during orienteering week."

"It's orientation week, you dick," Jarryd corrected straightaway. "He's not going tramping." Jarryd turned to him. "Your girlfriend must be bummed that you're going so far away, though?"

His whole body tensed. He glanced round. They were all waiting for him to answer. "Nah," he said and took a swig of beer. "I'm not seeing anyone at the moment."

A look of confusion flashed across Jarryd's face. "But what about the girl you were with the other night?"

Tom was on his feet before he had a chance to reply.

"Leave the poor guy alone, eh?" Tom said, and

disappeared into the house. Jarryd opened his mouth to respond but then thought better of it and continued with his dinner in silence.

At half past eleven, with only thirty minutes of the year remaining, they headed back down to the beach. Tom led the way, a box of fireworks under one arm.

Fortunately, it was a cloudless night. The moon hadn't risen yet, and the stars overhead sparkled like diamonds. The closer they got to the beach, the louder the thud of the waves grew.

"What's the time?" Amber shouted. She and Deano were walking several paces behind the group.

"Nearly quarter to," Jarryd turned and yelled back. "Hurry up, you two lovebirds, or we'll miss it."

The beach was empty save for one other group at the far end of the bay. Their laughter was amplified by the stillness of the night.

Sam stood and gazed quietly out to sea. Close to the shore, the water shimmered and frothed white on the crest of each wave, but further out, there was nothing but a single expanse of black. He strained his eyes to see the horizon, but it was hidden from view. The sand beneath his feet was surprisingly warm. He prodded the surface with his toes and felt the cool, silky layer just beneath the surface.

"Right, losers," Franklin called out to get everybody's attention. "By my watch, we have one minute to go."

Jarryd handed out the last of the beers, and they all huddled in a tight circle, their arms linked over each other's shoulders. By no design on his part, he found himself standing next to Tom. He could feel the weight of Tom's arm on the crook of his neck.

"Twenty, nineteen, eighteen," Franklin began, but before he got any further, there was a roar from the other end of the beach and a firework shot up into the sky. Simultaneously, the campground behind them sprang into life.

"My watch must be slow," Franklin said, looking at his wrist in disbelief. He tapped the glass face of the watch as if it would adjust the error.

"You're slow," Jarryd answered with a friendly shove and they all split apart.

"Happy New Year," they greeted one another. The guys clasped hands and patted each other on the back, while Amber kissed them each on the cheek. When nobody was watching, he reached up and touched his neck where Tom's arm had been.

"Let's get these fireworks under way, eh, Tommy?" Jarryd rubbed his palms together enthusiastically.

They stood and watched in silence as Tom tore open the box and removed the first rocket. He jabbed the wooden stake into the sand and motioned to them to stand back. There was a flash of light as the fuse ignited, followed by a pregnant pause and then the sudden whoosh of the rocket as it shot up into the air. It exploded with a loud bang. A cascade of red and green sparks floated gently down to earth.

"Wow-wee!" Amber shrieked like a child.

Tom launched another two rockets, and then Franklin demanded a turn.

"Do you want to light the last one?" Tom turned to him and held out a small rocket with the words *Sonic*

Boom printed on the side.

"Go on," Jarryd encouraged. "Amber's much too pretty to lose a hand."

He forced out a smile, took the firework and lighter from Tom, and strode several metres away from the group. The rocket secure in the sand, he squatted on his haunches to light the fuse.

With the other rockets, there had been a delay of at least ten seconds, but no sooner was the taper alight than the rocket let out a deafening squeal. In the same instant, the stake that the rocket was attached to tilted forward at a forty-five-degree angle.

He stumbled backwards with fright, tripped on his own feet, and landed on his back in the sand, as the rocket whizzed past his right ear. He opened his eyes in time to witness the explosion of colour over head.

"Now that's what I call a firework!" a voice shouted behind him.

Tom's face eclipsed the night sky. "Are you OK?"

He scrambled to his feet, brushing the sand off his clothes. "What the fuck happened?"

Jarryd and the others were killing themselves with laughter. He gritted his teeth to stop himself from saying something he would regret.

"Come on, let's head back, eh?" Tom said.

"I think I'll stay here a bit longer," he replied, more curtly than he had meant to. He knew the laughter wasn't malicious, but he was embarrassed nonetheless. Out of the corner of his eye, he saw Tom glare at Jarryd.

There was a moment of silence and then Jarryd shrugged. "Come on, guys. Let's go."

Tom turned to him. "Mind if I join you?" he asked, letting the others go on without him. Sam shook his head.

The beach was completely still, save for the rhythmic thud of the waves. Even the seagulls had retreated to the rocks to await the dawn. Tom sat down on the sand at his feet.

For a while, neither of them made any attempt to speak. He wrapped his arms around his shins and gazed into the darkness.

"Fancy going for a swim?" Tom asked at last.

He turned his head, and they made eye contact. He held Tom's gaze for a second and then looked down at his shorts. "I don't have my togs on."

A mischievous grin spread across Tom's face. "Who's going to see?"

Before he could reply, Tom was on his feet. He removed his T-shirt, screwed it into a ball and tossed it in his direction. It unravelled in midair and landed in a heap at his feet. "Come on." By the time Tom reached the water's edge, he was already down to his boxer shorts.

Surely he'll stop there? Sam thought as Tom slipped out of his undies and dropped them on the sand.

"What are you waiting for?" Tom grinned over his shoulder. "It's almost tropical in here." The goose bumps on his arse said otherwise, though. In one fluid motion, Tom dove beneath the waves and disappeared.

When Sam stepped into the water, he gasped involuntarily. "You liar!" he shouted into the darkness. "It's fucking freezing."

"Just dive in!" Tom yelled back. "It's warmer once you're in."

He took a deep breath and inched forward. He almost squealed like a stuck pig when the water reached his crotch, but he forced himself to continue. "Where are you?" he called out. It was impossible to see anything.

"Over here," Tom answered, somewhere off to his left. He sounded fairly close, though.

He didn't see the wave coming before it crashed right over his head. He came to the surface gasping for air, his nose and throat stinging from the saltwater.

Tom was by his side in a flash.

"I—" he spluttered as another wave washed over him. Tom grabbed hold of his elbow and held him up. He rubbed the water from his eyes with his fingertips. "I thought you said it would get warmer."

SAM LAY AWAKE. A thousand thoughts were racing through his mind. *Why had Tom invited him to come away with them? Were things serious between Tom and Eve? When would she be coming back? Was it possible to die from sexual frustration?* Just the thought of Tom—his broad shoulders, his narrow waist, the shape of his mouth and the small indentation at the cleft of his buttocks—made his body ache. *Or will I just go slowly insane?*

With a groan, he reached for his cellphone and flipped open the cover. The screen was so bright that he had to squint to read the time. Eight minutes past three. The New Year was only a few hours old. He rolled over to face the wall and pulled the covers up under his chin.

It was amazing how much noise an old house could make, even in the dead of night. A ticking clock, a dripping tap, the drone of a refrigerator. He held his breath and listened to the sound of silence. Outside somewhere an owl hooted.

When the floorboards in the hall creaked, he didn't think anything of it. The bathroom light had pinged on a short while before. One of the other guys probably needed to use the toilet now. He waited for the familiar tinkle of water on porcelain, but it never came and the bathroom light remained off.

You must be hearing things, he told himself. The next thing he knew, it was morning.

TOM JUST COULDN'T get comfortable; whichever way he lay, sleep eluded him.

It was pointless pretending that he hadn't wanted something to happen back there on the beach. Although he had to admit that if Sam had made a move, he probably would have run a mile.

The mattress was half deflated, and as he rolled over, his elbow and hipbone jabbed into the hard ground.

"Fuck," he cursed, and sat up, his head brushing against the fabric roof of the tent. God, he hated tenting.

He crawled out into the fresh air and made his way across the lawn, towards to the house. His sleeping bag trailed behind him through the dewy grass.

It was silent inside the bach, and the moonlight pouring in through the lounge window lent the living room an otherworldly feel. He walked over to the sofa and shook out his sleeping bag. On the wall opposite, the clock was making a loud ticking sound, but he was so tired that he doubted anything could keep him from sleep. He climbed into the sleeping bag, punched one of the grubby scatter cushions into shape, and lay his head down.

From where he was lying, he had an unobstructed view of Sam's bedroom door. It was open a crack, but the room within was cloaked in darkness.

Deep down, he knew he had been playing with fire inviting Sam to come away with them. Yet it had given him a thrill when Sam said yes. And now that they were here, removed from the real world, he wished they could stay longer.

An hour later, he was no closer to falling asleep. With a sigh, he rolled onto his back and stared up at the ceiling. *I should be missing Eve*, he thought, feeling a pang of guilt. But he didn't miss her, no matter how much he tried to convince himself that he did. All he could think about was Sam.

He pulled the cushion out from under his head, held it down over his face, and groaned.

You've got a girlfriend. She's gorgeous, and everyone likes her. Don't screw it all up over something that can never be.

SAM EMERGED FROM his room the next morning looking as if he had been pulled through a hedge backwards. He had finally drifted off shortly before five, only to be woken an hour and a half later by Tom and Jarryd crashing about outside. As soon as they had driven off, he got out of bed.

"You look as good as I feel," Amber said when he appeared in the kitchen doorway. She was buttering herself a piece of toast. The sweet smell turned his stomach.

"Is that coffee?" he said, dropping onto the nearest

chair and cradling his head in his arms.

"Yeah. I just made it. Did you want some?"

He said yes without raising his head.

"What are your plans for the day?" Amber asked. She placed a mug of steaming coffee by his head. The aroma was overpowering. He sat up and took a sip.

"Thanks. I'm not sure." Outside, the sky was a perfect blue. It was going to be another stunning day. "I might go for a swim. Did Tom say what time they'd be back?"

Amber shrugged her shoulders. "If the surf is up, I don't imagine we'll see them until later this arvo."

He was lying on his bed reading when Tom and Jarryd arrived back. Amber had been right on the money; it was four thirty in the afternoon. He heard a car door slam and a minute later Tom appeared in the doorway.

"Hey, how's it going?"

"Yeah, not bad," he replied. "How was the surf?"

"Awesome, thanks. There was a good swell."

Tom had a look on his face that made him feel slightly uneasy. "I was going to have a beer," Tom said. "Do you want one?"

He had been waiting all day to see Tom. Several times he had jumped up, certain that he had heard Tom's car pull up, only to meet with disappointment. "Yeah, sure," he said casually, "I'll be out in a minute."

Tom lingered for a moment, as if there was something else he wanted to say, and then turned and walked away.

chapter eight

"CAN I ASK a question?"

Tom swallowed his last mouthful of butter chicken and put down his fork. He took a large gulp of beer and wiped his mouth on a square of handy towel. He screwed the paper cloth into a ball and dropped it onto his empty plate. "Depends what it is."

"How did you know that Sam was the one?" Olivia had already finished eating but was still picking at the plastic containers in the middle of the table. She tore off a piece of roti bread and wiped it round her plate to soak up the last of the sauce.

"Why do you ask that?" He took another sip of beer and eyed her over the rim of the glass.

"I was just wondering. That's all."

He hadn't been expecting company for dinner, but when Olivia turned up unannounced, it wasn't a surprise. For a few weeks now, she had been dropping in at random times of the day. He suspected that Carla was behind the 'impromptu' visits.

"I don't know," he answered after a long pause. Olivia tilted her head to one side. She reached across the table for his beer.

"Hey," he protested, but she paid no attention. If Carla found out that he was allowing her sixteen-year-old daughter to drink, she would hit the roof.

"Did you always know you were gay?"

He fixed her with a stare. "Where's this all coming from?" he asked, one eyebrow raised. But she just shrugged and took another sip from the glass. He walked over to the fridge for a fresh bottle of beer. He poured the contents into a glass and sat back down at the table.

"The day I met Sam," he said. "I mean, that's when I knew for sure." He leaned back in his seat and linked his hands behind his head. "My girlfriend wasn't over the moon about it, though."

He didn't think he had ever seen Olivia lost for words before. Her jaw almost hit the table. "I see your mum never told you about Eve, then?"

Olivia shook her head. She picked up the glass and realised it was empty.

"There's another in the fridge, but I'm having half—OK? I don't want your mum finding out I got you pissed."

It was obvious that Olivia was itching to ask questions but didn't know quite where to begin.

"Spit it out," he said, taking the bottle away from her before she emptied its entire contents into her glass.

"You and—"

"Eve."

"Did you ever—you know?"

He shifted uncomfortably in the chair and glanced out the window. It was dark outside and the brightness of the room made it impossible to see the surrounding bush. He could hear the wind howling from the north, whipping the rain against the windows in gusts. "I'm not sure that's the type of thing you're meant to ask an uncle, but for the record, yes, we did."

"But how?" It was clear she hadn't meant to voice what she was thinking. Her face went bright red.

He stood up and took a bottle of vodka down from the shelf above the fridge. He was going to need something stronger than beer. "I thought your mum would've had that conversation with you by now," he teased. He knew exactly what Olivia meant but he didn't feel like making it easy for her. "When a man loves a woman—"

"Not that," Olivia interrupted. He turned away before she caught him smiling.

He dropped a handful of ice cubes into a short glass, doused them with a generous slug of vodka, and topped it up with soda. He took a large sip and steeled himself for the conversation he was about to have. Like her mother, Olivia would never settle for half-answers. He raised both eyebrows, as if to say "Continue."

"Well, it's just, for women it's not essential—"

He gave her a questioning look.

"I mean, if you don't find a guy attractive—it doesn't mean you can't—" she continued in a roundabout way and then sighed. "Do you know what I mean?"

"I thought I did, but I'm not sure I do any more."

He had never been as relieved to see Carla as he was when she walked into the room.

"What's going on here?" Carla said, looking from him to the glass of beer in Olivia's hand. "Are you letting her drink? Christ, Tom, she's only sixteen."

Carla marched over to Olivia and snatched the glass out of her hand before turning and giving her brother a look that could kill.

"Where's Nathan?" he said, trying to change the subject. Almost on cue, his eight-year-old nephew appeared in the doorway, behind his mother. He was holding a tablet computer. His eyes were glued to the screen.

"Hi, Nathan," he said, but Nathan didn't look up.

"Nathan!" Carla scolded and snatched the device out of his hands. "Answer when your uncle is talking to you."

His nephew glanced up from beneath a thick mop of blond hair and smiled. For the first time, he saw what everybody else did; it was like looking at a photograph of himself at the same age.

Carla dropped her handbag onto the kitchen bench, took a glass out of the cupboard, and, without saying a word, poured herself a drink. There was a small square of roti left on the plate in the middle of the table. She picked it up and popped it into her mouth. "Christ, I'm hungry." She turned to Olivia. "Your father is taking you and Nate out for the day tomorrow."

Olivia started to protest, but Carla cut her off. "I don't want to hear it right now. He's picking you up at nine o'clock."

"I'm not going," Olivia glared at her mother.

"You're going, and that's the end of it."

"She's just jealous," Nathan piped up all of a sudden. He was still tapping away on the tablet again, but, clearly, he had been listening to every word.

"Jealous?" Carla repeated. They all turned towards Nathan.

"Of Dad's new girlfriend," he said, without even looking up.

It was hard to describe the expression on Carla's face. She looked shocked, disgusted, and amused all at once.

"I am not jealous," Olivia protested, but nobody was listening any more. The cat had chosen the same moment to make his grand entrance. He rubbed his face against the leg of Tom's chair as he trotted past, and then, once everybody was watching, plopped down in the centre of the room and started to lick his bum.

"Eew." Nathan screwed his face up.

"Bentley, that's disgusting," Tom said, and shooed the cat out of the room. "Nathan, take Bentley to the laundry and fill up his biscuits, please."

"Is he right?" Carla asked Olivia as soon as Nathan was out of earshot. "That Dad's got a new girlfriend?"

Olivia looked increasingly uncomfortable. She shrugged her shoulders. "I guess."

"How long has it been going on?" Carla continued to probe, but Olivia snapped, "Why do you care? It's not like you wanted him."

There was a long, awkward silence before Nathan reappeared. He was clutching one hand in the other. "Bentley scratched me."

Carla prised the hand away from his body to take a look. The wound was only surface deep. "Olivia, take your brother to the bathroom, please, and help him put a plaster on his hand." Olivia made a loud huffing sound, but she did as she was told.

"I take it you didn't know about the girlfriend," Tom said once they were alone.

Carla rolled her eyes. "Not about this one, no."

He got to his feet and started to tidy away the empty takeaway containers. "And you—are you jealous?"

Carla laughed. "No, I wouldn't have Adam back if he was gift-wrapped." She sighed. "But sometimes I think it'd be nice to have someone to talk to."

He suddenly felt a pang of guilt. For months, he had been so consumed with his own grief that he had forgotten that his sister was raising two children by herself.

"You can talk to me," he said. Carla smiled and gave his arm a squeeze.

He stacked the last of the dirty plates into the dishwasher and then wiped down the benchtop.

"Come on, it's time we were going," Carla said as soon as Nate returned. She placed her hands on the table and pushed herself to her feet with a groan. "Where's your sister?"

Nate shrugged, but the familiar low-pitched drone of headphones indicated that she wasn't far away.

Tom tossed the used tea towel into the sink and followed them out of the room. Olivia was standing in the hall, leaning against the door jamb. Without looking up from her smartphone, she followed her brother out to the car.

When they reached the door, Carla turned and put her arms around him. A good twenty centimetres shorter than Tom, her head only came up to his chest. He wasn't one for public displays of affection, and he felt his muscles tense.

"What are you playing at?"

"Just shut up and put your arms around me," Carla replied, resting her head against his breast. "It'll be OK, you know. The grief won't last for ever."

"Mm-hm," he replied, obediently linking his arms behind her back and resting his chin on the top of her head.

The moment was shattered by the sound of raised voices outside. Carla stood back and, holding him firmly by the arms, looked him straight in the eye. She smiled and gave his arms a squeeze. "Wanna swap with me for a bit?"

He laughed and shook his head. "I'll call you tomorrow," he called after her, but she didn't respond; she already had other fish to fry.

chapter nine

IT WAS DARK by the time they pulled up outside his parents' house. He was already several hours later than he'd said he would be.

"I hope you don't get into too much trouble." Tom spoke quietly so as not to wake the others, who had been asleep since before Masterton. A lorry had jack-knifed just north of the brewery at Mangatainoka and the traffic jam had backed up as far as Woodville.

"I'll be fine," he replied, unfolding himself from the back seat and removing his backpack from the mass of belongings in the boot. He walked round to the driver's window, which was open. "Thanks for the ride," he said, delaying the goodbye for as long as he reasonably could. "I had a nice time."

"Me too." Tom looked up at him and smiled.

"I guess I'll see you round then," he said, and kicked the tarmac with the toe of his shoe.

Tom looked in the rear-view mirror. The others were still dead to the world. "Of course."

Reluctantly, he turned away. There was nothing left to say.

Patch was at the door before his key was in the lock. Two nostrils flared behind the frosted glass pane. He reached down to stop Patch from escaping as he opened the door.

"Sam, is that you?" a voice called out of the dark.

He let the door swing shut behind him and dropped his bag on the floor. "Yes, Mum."

The hall light flicked on as his mother stepped out of the bedroom. She gently closed the door behind her. "Why on earth are you so late? I've been out of my mind with worry."

She rushed forward to give him a kiss and then sniffed at the air. "Have you been drinking?" she asked, The furrows on her forehead deepened. "Actually, on second thoughts, don't tell me. I don't think I want to know. There's some food in the fridge if you want it. Your father has already gone to bed."

"Thanks," he smiled. "There was a crash." He saw her eyes grow wide with alarm and quickly added, "It was nothing to do with us, but it caused a long traffic jam." He reached down and scratched Patch behind the ears, who was sniffing inquisitively at his pants.

"Well, so long as you're OK," his mother said. She squeezed him on the arm and turned back towards the bedroom. "'Night."

As he slowly undressed, he dropped the dirty clothes one by one into the laundry basket. Then he opened the wardrobe and stood naked in front of the full-length mirror inside.

He sucked in his stomach and drew back his shoulders to inflate his chest. He held the posture for a moment

142

and then exhaled deeply. It was hard to identify with the man's body reflected back at him in the glass. Inside, he still felt like an oversized kid. The idea that another human being could find his body attractive was somewhat absurd.

He climbed into bed and closed his eyes. Yet he was far from sleep. All he could think about was Tom. He pictured Tom's smile and felt an invisible hand squeeze his heart.

He rolled onto his side. The bedsheets were fresh and felt like silk against his skin. He slid an arm beneath the cool underside of his pillow. He buried his face in the pillow to muffle the sound and let out a deep groan. How would he be able to concentrate on anything else ever again?

He kept his head down as he jogged along the footpath towards the beach. The wind had changed direction overnight and was blowing from the south again, dusting the front yards of the houses along the foreshore with coarse, yellow sand. As he looked up to cross the road, a gust of wind caught him full in the face.

"Fuck," he cursed, slowing to a walk and rubbing the grit from his eyes. Unfortunately, he drove the grains of sand only deeper., so that by the time he reached the bay, tears were streaming down his cheeks and his eye sockets felt like two raw pits in the front of his head. He made straight for the drinking fountain outside the surf club and splashed fresh water over his face. He sighed with relief.

As soon as he was able to see again, he went inside

and climbed the wooden staircase up to the café on the first floor. Holly was already there, waiting at a table by the window.

"You took your time," she said.

He smiled sheepishly and sat down at the seat opposite.

From where they were sitting, they had an unrestricted view of the beach. Holly looked out the window at the waves crashing on the sand below. The usually raucous seagulls were clustered together in tight groups, their heads retracted deep into their bodies.

He reached into his pocket and took out a packet of cigarettes. He offered the packet to Holly but she shook her head. "I thought you were going to give up for New Year."

"Yeah, well, maybe next year."

Although it was midsummer, it was actually warmer inside the surf club than it was outside. For several days now, an Antarctic blast had been buffeting the capital, making it feel more like August than January.

"I'll have a flat white," Holly ordered once the waitress appeared, "with two sugars." He waved away the menu and asked for the same.

Holly leaned across the table conspiratorially when they were alone. "So tell me all about it."

He shrugged and looked out the window again. "There's nothing much to tell."

A ferry was inching its way out from behind the rocks that concealed the entrance to the harbour. He waited until the stern was in full view before he turned back to Holly.

144

He stubbed out his cigarette and reached automatically for another but Holly snatched the packet away. "Not until you've spilled the beans. I want to know all the gory details."

"I told you, nothing happened."

"But you wanted it to?"

His mouth twitched up at the corners as if by reflex.

"I knew it!" Holly exclaimed. The woman at the next table turned and looked in their direction.

"Shush, will you," Sam said.

In the time that it took for their drinks to arrive, the tide advanced several metres up the beach. He watched the white-capped waves creeping closer.

"Well?" Holly was staring at him above the rim of her coffee cup.

"For a moment, I thought that maybe—" He let the words trail off. He took a sip of his drink before he continued. "But then I found out he's got a girlfriend. A hot girlfriend."

Holly's face sank.

They finished their drinks in silence.

"Come on—let's get out of here, eh," he mumbled, searching his pockets for some money. He found a crumpled five-dollar note, which he flattened out and tossed into the centre of the table.

"Do you think you'll ever tell your folks you're gay?" Holly asked as they walked on up the beach. Thankfully, there was nobody round to hear her motor mouth.

"No way. They'd never accept it."

"You don't know that," Holly replied. "The world's moved on. People don't care so much any more."

"I can assure you that my folks will most certainly care.

Holly seemed to mull over what he had just said. "Well, I guess you don't need to tell them for a while anyway." She reached into her pocket for a stick of gum. "Want some?"

"Ta," he said, removing the foil wrapper and popping the rectangular wafer into his mouth. He snapped it in half with his tongue.

By the time he arrived home, his mother was putting the finishing touches to the Sunday lunch. The whole house smelt of roast lamb, and within seconds, his stomach was rumbling loudly.

"Lunch won't be long. Can you set the table, please?" his mother asked, giving the roast potatoes a shake before returning them to the oven.

He hung his jacket on the hook by the front door and moved silently to the dresser, where the placemats were kept.

"Where have you been today?" his mother asked.

"For a walk," he replied. He purposely left out the fact that Holly had been with him. His mother still hadn't forgiven her for the magazine incident. He retrieved the salt and pepper from the pantry and placed them in the centre of the table.

His mother was standing with her back to him, but as she turned towards the sink to drain the vegetables, he saw the red lump on the side of her face.

"Mum, what happened?"

She didn't reply, but the tensing of her shoulders under her blouse told him enough.

"The bastard," he swore.

She placed the pot on the kitchen bench and turned to face him. He could see that she had tried to mask the bruise with make-up, but the bluish tinge was still visible.

"Please don't, Sam," she said. "It'll only make things worse."

He didn't answer her. He wasn't sure what to say. Had it been the first time, he might have believed there was something that he could do.

"I wish he was dead," he said under his breath, but loud enough for her to hear. He saw her recoil.

"Don't say such a thing. He is still your father."

"How can you defend him?" he asked incredulously. He clenched and unclenched his fists; he could feel himself getting angry. His mother turned back to the sink and picked up the pot.

"He's been under a lot of pressure lately. He doesn't mean it. He just doesn't know how to deal with his emotions."

Before he was able to reply, the front door opened.

"What's going on?" his sister asked, stepping cautiously into the kitchen. She looked from him to his mother and then back to him.

"Ask Mum," he replied, pushing past her and out into the hall.

"Sam, where are you going?" his mother yelled after him. "Lunch is almost ready."

"I'm not hungry!" he shouted, slamming the front door behind him.

His father was sitting at the kitchen table when he returned. He had been pacing the streets for the best part

147

of an hour, trying to work out whom he was most angry
with: his father, or his mother for putting up with him.

"Would you like something to eat?" his mother asked.
She was out of her seat before he could reply. She
retrieved his lunch from the oven, where she had been
keeping it warm.

"Seen Tom lately?" his father asked, shaking out the
newspaper as he turned the page.

He froze, the fork suspended in midair. "No," he
replied warily, "not since New Year's."

His father folded the newspaper in half and then in
half again. He read in silence for a minute before he put
the paper down. "I suppose we might as well go for a
drink when you're finished."

Sam felt like telling his father to fuck off, that he would
rather stick pins in his eyes than drink with him right
now, but he kept his mouth shut. It was the perfect
excuse to see Tom.

"I'm talking to you," his father said when he still
hadn't replied.

"Yeah, OK, thanks," he mumbled through a mouthful
of food.

"There's a few things I want to talk to you about."

He finished chewing and swallowed. "What things?"

His father put down his knife and fork and leaned
back in his chair. He heard the wood creak under the
strain. "Let's just say there's a few grounds rules that
need to be set before you go off running amok down
there at the university."

Sam shifted uneasily and took a sip of water. He kept
his eyes down.

"I know what young lads are like," his father continued. Across the table, his sister croaked with suppressed laughter. His father reached for a slice of bread, coated it liberally with butter, and folded it in half. "I used to be one," he said, taking a bite.

His father eyed him suspiciously while he chewed. When he had finished, he wiped his mouth with his napkin, dropped it onto the empty plate and pushed back his chair. "Don't go getting any girls in trouble, is all I wanted to say on the matter."

This time, he almost laughed out loud. "No, Dad. I promise I won't."

His father looked at him, as if he were unsure whether he was being mocked or not. "Very well, then," he grunted. "Get your coat. It's cold out," he added, striding out of the room.

"Don't forget I'm taking you to the university bookshop tomorrow," his mother reminded him as he followed his father out the door. He knew it was her way of saying, "Please don't stay out late."

They walked in silence. His father kept half a stride ahead the whole way.

"The usual?" Ngaire asked as soon as they walked through the door. She was sitting in her usual spot at the end of the bar, a cigarette hanging from her mouth. He wondered whether she ever moved.

His father nodded. "And whatever you're having." She smiled, revealing a scattering of yellow teeth.

He scanned the empty room. There was no sign of Tom, Jarryd, or any of the others.

"Here you go, son." Ngaire slopped two jugs of pale ale on the counter in front of him and returned to her seat. His father was already talking to a group of old guys huddled round a leaner in the corner.

For over an hour, he stood beside his father in silence. Every time the door swung open, his heart leapt into his throat, so that by the time Jarryd walked through the door, he felt mentally exhausted.

He stood up straight and tried to look as relaxed as possible. With Jarryd now here, Tom wouldn't be far behind. He took a sip of warm beer to loosen his dry throat. Right on cue, the door opened again and in walked Tom.

He took a step forward and froze, the breath knocked out of him.

Standing beside Tom was a girl he didn't recognise—though he knew who she was instantly; Amber had described her in painstaking detail. She really was as attractive as he had feared.

"I'm back for a month," her voice carried across the room. "I surprised him," she giggled. He almost flinched when she kissed Tom on the cheek. He took a step backward, towards the bar.

"You all right, boy?" Ngaire was wiping down the bar with a dirty cloth.

He turned and gave her a blank look. He couldn't think straight.

"You don't look too good," she said.

"I'm OK, thanks. I just need some fresh air."

Ngaire shrugged and continued with her chores.

He slipped behind his father and out the door without saying a word. He kept his head down until he was clear of the building.

THE NEXT FEW weeks were, without doubt, the worst of his life.

"Are you sure you're not coming down with something?" His mother leaned over the bed and placed a hand on his forehead. She held it there for a moment, her eyebrows knitted together in concern. "You don't feel hot," she said, somewhat accusatorily.

It was nine o'clock in the morning, and, for once, there was nowhere he needed to be.

"I'm just tired. I didn't sleep well last night."

He rolled onto his back and pulled the covers up under his chin. He stared up at the ceiling. There was a crack in the plaster. He was sure it hadn't been there before the last earthquake, a month or so before.

"Well, don't forget your gran and grandad are coming for tea tonight. They want to see you before you leave." She turned and walked out of the room.

Immediately the door was closed, he threw back the covers and jumped out of bed. It had taken him days to make up his mind, and now that he had resolved to see Tom one last time, he wasn't going to let anything stand in his way.

Tom wasn't at home, and since his flatmate had no idea when he would be home, he decided not to wait. Next he tried the rugby club, only to find all the doors locked and the lights turned off. He stood by the kerb and tried to think of where to try next. Only one other place sprang to mind.

When he reached the beach and saw Tom's ute parked up outside the surf club, he breathed a sigh of relief. He quickly scanned the shore, but there was only one person out on the water and he was far too short to be Tom.

He leaned against the wall of the club and waited for Tom to materialise. Twenty minutes later, though, there was still no sign of him.

Sam folded his arms and hunched his shoulders against the cold. He would have to make his up mind soon: either to go in and find Tom or to leave. Right now, he felt inclined to leave, but a voice inside his head told him he would regret it if he did.

He took a deep breath and stepped inside.

The dimly lit foyer was empty. He looked round, unsure what to do next. The staircase that led up to the café was cloaked in darkness. Clearly, Tom wasn't up there.

Should he wait where he was or try one of the two doors on the ground floor? He took a step towards the doors and stopped. If he was caught nosing around a place he wasn't supposed to be, he could get into trouble.

He was still trying to decide what to do when the door to his left swung open. A guy he didn't recognise walked past without giving him so much as a second look.

"Hey," he called out without thinking. The guy stopped and turned. "Sorry," he continued. "You haven't seen Tom around, have you?"

The guy motioned to the door he had just walked through. "Yeah, bro. He's through there."

Sam took a step towards the blue door, and stopped. His heart was beating so fast he thought he might actually faint. *What good can come of this?* a voice inside his head whispered. It sounded quite a lot like his mother's.

152

He shook his head to clear his thoughts before continuing.

It was much brighter on the other side of the door and it took his eyes a moment to adjust to the light. The room was empty, save for a solitary pile of clothes on a bench in the far corner. He recognised Tom's coat hanging from a hook on the wall.

He held his breath and scanned the room. His heart was in his throat. He half expected Tom to appear from nowhere, like some sort of apparition. At the far end of the changing room, there was another door, and judging by the sound of running water, it led to the showers.

The pipes above his head clunked as the water was shut off. He stood motionless, his eyes transfixed on the empty doorway. *It had better be Tom in there*, he thought; otherwise, he would have some serious explaining to do. The long silence was broken only by the squelch of footsteps on the tiled floor.

He gulped when Tom appeared. He wasn't wearing a thing. Tom wandered slowly across the room, right towards where he was standing. His face was hidden beneath the towel he was using to dry his hair.

Sam had seen Tom's naked body once before, but that had been under cover of darkness. Now, the artificial light illuminated every detail.

He had left it far too long to make his presence known. Still, he knew that he had to do something, and fast. He coughed, unable to think of anything better. The sound echoed off the concrete walls.

Tom spun round. He snatched the towel from his head and held it in front of waist. But when he saw who it was, he exhaled with relief. "Sam, you scared the crap out of me."

He felt his face flush with shame. He had made a terrible error of judgment.

"Sorry," he mumbled, taking a step back, towards the door. "I came—" he began, but stopped. He took a deep breath. "I wanted to say goodbye."

Tom moved forward, closing the gap between them. "When do you leave?"

"Tomorrow." He kept his eyes to the floor.

"Oh," Tom said. "Have you got time for a drink?"

He looked up and smiled nervously. "I think I'd better go."

Without saying a word, Tom closed the gap between them.

Sam could feel his heart hammering against the inside of his ribcage. It was beating dangerously fast. He thought about running but knew his legs wouldn't cooperate if he tried. Tom was standing so close now that he could smell the faint aroma of shampoo.

"Goodbye, then," Tom said, his voice almost a whisper. He had a strange glint in his eye.

Sam was immobilised by fear. He looked up, as if for help, but Tom just smiled.

When Tom reached out and touched his face, it felt as if an electric current was surging through him. Every muscle in his body trembled.

Tom's lips were surprisingly soft. Tom kissed him gently at first—quick, tentative. But passion soon got the better of both of them. He pushed his body against Tom's and felt an unmistakable hardness against his stomach.

Tom let go of the towel and it fell to the floor. Slowly, Tom's left arm moved around his waist, his fingertips working their way down his spine until they came to rest just above the hollow of his back. A shiver shot through his body, and he let out a squeak.

"Ticklish, eh?" Tom whispered in his ear. Tom's breath brushed the sensitive skin on his neck, which made him squirm all the more. Without waiting for a reply, Tom covered his mouth with his own, his teeth nipping playfully at his lower lip.

He felt himself melting away fast; if he didn't put a stop to this now, he would never be able to leave. Summoning all the strength he had left, he put his palms on Tom's chest and pushed him away. "Stop," he mumbled. It sounded more like a request than an order. But it had the desired effect. Tom tensed and he pulled away. "What's wrong?"

He hadn't meant to laugh. Tom winced as if he had just slapped him round the face.

"*What's wrong?*" He repeated Tom's question. "I'm leaving in less than twelve hours. And you have a girlfriend." The last sentence came out more acerbically than he had intended. Tom turned away.

He stopped and looked back before opening the door to the foyer. Tom was still standing with his back to him.

"Bye," he said quietly, but Tom didn't answer.

THE HOUSE WAS a hive of activity the following morning. His father had already filled the car with gas by the time he surfaced and was now dragging his trunk down the hallway, towards the door. "You'd better get a move on," he said, letting the trunk drop to the floor with a crash. Thank God there wasn't anything breakable inside. "The ferry won't wait for you."

"Sam, get into that shower now," his mother said, emerging from the kitchen and squeezing past him into his room. She reappeared a moment later, his used bed linen screwed up in a ball under one arm. She sighed with exasperation. "I'm leaving in twenty minutes—with or without you."

He stood in the shower and let the steaming water cascade over his face and body. He hadn't got a wink of sleep all night and his joints ached with tiredness.

He closed his eyes and tried again to piece together what had happened at the surf club. Gaps were already appearing in his memory.

After leaving the changing room, he had headed straight for the far end of the beach. He had sat on the rocks, facing directly into the southerly, until he had lost all feeling in his fingers and toes. He couldn't really remember the walk home.

He climbed out of the shower and dried himself with a towel. The clock on the wall was ticking loudly, and for a moment he paused to watch the second hand as it moved, unstoppably, round the face.

"Sam, get a move on!" his mother yelled through the door, jerking him back to reality.

She was already sitting behind the wheel when he walked into the front yard. His father was standing next to the driver's door. "Don't drive too fast," he heard his father lecturing her. "And watch out for the cops." His father rapped twice on the roof of the car and walked back towards the house without saying a word to him.

"Get in, Sam," his mother said through the open window. She leaned across to pop the lock on the passenger door, and he slipped in beside her. "Ignore him. He's sad you're leaving. He just doesn't know how to say it."

The car was full to bursting. His trunk took up most of the back seat. Anything that wouldn't fit inside had been draped over the top, leaving barely enough room for his mother to see through the back window. The disassembled pieces of his bike had been crammed into every available space.

His mother turned the key in the ignition and the engine spluttered into life. Using both hands, she released the handbrake and they rolled forward through the gate. It was an old car and weighed as much as a small tank. As she tugged on the steering wheel, her cheeks flushed with colour. A pump of the gas pedal propelled them up the small dip in the gutter and out onto the road.

When they reached the end of the street, he glanced one last time in the wing mirror. A motorbike was approaching from the other direction. His heart leapt into his throat. But before he had a chance to see who was riding, they rounded the corner and the street disappeared from view. He slumped back into the seat and rested his forehead on the window, the warmth of his breath misting up the glass.

chapter ten

TOM SAT IN the car park and watched the crowd at the door disperse. He hadn't touched a golf club in over six months, but this morning he woke up itching to get out on the course. He had been cooped up inside for far too long.

Hurry up, he thought, glancing at the two old guys lingering by the entrance to the club. He had been hoping to sneak out to the first tee without anyone noticing. He wasn't ready to cope with other people's sympathy just yet.

Once the coast was clear, he climbed out of the car and unloaded his clubs from the boot. He didn't bother assembling the trolley; he was planning on doing nine holes only. He hoisted the bag onto his shoulder and turned towards the club.

"Tom!" Mrs Murdoch screeched as soon as he walked through the door. She came waddling down the hall towards him, a pile of folded towels under one arm. At no more than a metre thirty, she was as wide as she was tall. "It's lovely to see you."

She put the towels on a nearby chair and pulled him

into a bear hug. Her face barely reached his stomach. He looked down at the crown of her head and couldn't help but notice the grey roots that were coming through.

"How are you?" she asked, grasping him firmly by the hands and stepping back to look him up and down. She cocked her head to one side, as if she were contemplating an invalid. He felt his body tense.

"I'm fine," he started to answer but she cut him off. "Stan, get out here!" she yelled over her shoulder, towards the office. "Tom's here."

The sound of Stan's grumbling was impossible to ignore. Mrs Murdoch rolled her eyes and told him not to take it personally. He didn't tell her that, right now, he felt a strange sort of affinity with her long-suffering husband.

Mr and Mrs Murdoch made for the most unlikely couple—one outgoing, the other taciturn. And while Stan was tall and lean, his wife was verging on being a midget. The logistics of their love-making flashed through his mind, and he blinked away the disturbing thought.

"G'day, Stan," he smiled, offering the old club manager his hand.

"Hello, Tom."

Stan Murdoch wasn't one to smile at the drop of a hat, but when he did, his whole face lit up. "It's really nice to see you," Stan said, and patted him on the shoulder. He was genuinely moved by the sincerity of the gesture.

"I see you've brought your clubs with you," Stan continued. He nodded at the bag next to him. "I assume you're looking to play a spot of golf today."

"I haven't booked, I'm afraid. It was a kind of last-minute decision."

"No worries, no worries." Stan waved away the apology. "I'm sure we can squeeze you in. Do you mind playing in a group?"

"Of course he doesn't mind," Mrs Murdoch answered on his behalf. She squeezed past her husband, into the office, and took possession of the leather-bound diary that recorded all the tee times. She ran a sausage-like finger down the page, her eyebrows drawing together as if she were trying to solve a difficult puzzle.

"Actually, Mrs Murdoch," he dared to interrupt her, "I would really like to play alone today. I'm not much—"

He was going to say "company" but she cut him off before he could finish the sentence.

"Now, there's a group of three about to tee off. I can add you in. You know them, to be sure. It's Brian Johnston and his two boys."

Mr Murdoch, who had been hovering in the doorway until now, stepped into the office and took the diary out from beneath his wife's nose. "Now, dear, Tom says he wants to play alone, and alone he shall play. So long as you don't mind waiting twenty minutes." He looked up over the top of his reading glasses and Tom was reminded of a teacher he had known at high school.

"Not at all," he replied with a grateful sigh. Out the corner of his eye, he saw Mrs Murdoch bristle. "Perhaps I could have a cup of tea while I'm waiting, though?" He smiled at her over her husband's shoulder and her face brightened immediately.

As he approached the first hole, he felt his stomach

lurch. It was as if somebody had reached into his abdomen and was twisting his insides for all they were worth. He paused, took a couple of deep breaths, and readjusted the bag on his shoulder before he continued. Golf was a game played largely in the mind. If he could just get past the first hole, he knew he would be OK.

He had played the course hundreds of times before. If he tried, he could probably get the ball onto the first green with his eyes closed. But now he wondered whether he would ever be able to tee off again without wanting to vomit.

"Will you just listen to what I'm telling you?" He would never forget the look that Sam had given him as he snatched the golf club out of his hand. He cringed at the memory.

Instead of teeing off, he took a moment to gather his thoughts. Without his having to asking, Stan had pushed back the next group's start time by a quarter of an hour. "Give you a bit of peace," Stan had said, slapping him gently on the back as they walked out the double doors, into the sunshine.

In the month following Sam's death, his sister had insisted he speak with a counsellor—post-traumatic stress, she had called it. He had told her, in no uncertain terms, just what he thought of the idea, but she had gone ahead and made an appointment anyway.

"Embrace your grief," the counsellor had told him. "Don't run from your feelings." Had he embraced his feelings at that particular moment, he would have punched her in the face. He didn't tell her this, however.

He closed his eyes and breathed in deeply through his

nose. Barely a year had passed, yet it was all still crystal clear in his memory—the way Sam had huffed and snatched the club back, the frustrated roll of the eyes he had given him in return. There was a reason partners weren't the ideal instructors.

"Don't hold it so—"

"Will you stop nagging me!"

"Just listen—"

He had barely had time to jump out of the way before the head of the club had flown past his face. It had come back down with an impressive whoosh of air but the ball had remained untouched on its wooden tee.

"—to me." He had finished the sentence between gritted teeth. When he had held out his hand for the club, Sam had thrown it back at him. He had reached down and picked it up off the ground without saying a word.

"Keep your left hand firm, but don't squeeze the club to death."

He knew he had hit a blinder just by the sound of the club connecting with the ball. He shielded his eyes with one hand and watched as the ball sailed down the fairway.

As Sam stepped up to the mark, placed his ball on the tee and went through his set-up routine, he had wanted to tell him to bring his arms closer together but he had thought better of it.

Sam had actually started promisingly, his head, shoulders and arms in the correct position, but on the downswing, he had lost it. His head had pulled upwards and the face of the club, instead of skimming the grass and coming up under the tee, had grazed the top of the ball and sent it scudding along the ground into the rough. Sam had stomped off before he could say anything.

They were at opposite ends of the fairway when it happened. From where he was standing, next to the green, it looked as if Sam had fainted. One minute he was standing upright; the next his knees buckled and he went down like a sack of potatoes.

Sam had been out cold for a good five minutes and was still only semi-conscious when they had stretchered him into the back of the ambulance. He didn't say a word all the way to the hospital, but just as they were turning off Adelaide Road into the hospital car park, he had opened his eyes and groaned.

"What is it?" Tom had asked, jumping to his feet and leaning over him.

"My hand," Sam had mumbled, turning his head to the side and opening his eyes just a crack. "You're crushing my fingers." He had almost elbowed the paramedic as he jerked his hand away.

He couldn't help but smile at the memory.

The paramedics had ferried Sam into a cubicle within the main triage ward and had hooked him up to a monitoring machine before disappearing for what felt like an eternity.

"How are we feeling now, Mr Wilson?" The curtain screening their cubicle was whipped back and a doctor in green scrubs appeared. He ignored Tom completely as he unhooked the clipboard from the end of the bed and scanned through Sam's notes. Sam had slumped forward in the bed, his chin resting on his chest.

"He took a golf ball to the head, doctor."

"I see." The doctor put down the clipboard and leaned over the bed. He pulled Sam's left eyelid back with his thumb and shone a bright light in his pupil. "Hmm," he mumbled to himself and then checked the right eye.

"Is everything OK?" Tom had asked. He had been unable to mask the concern in his voice. Sam looked up and gave them both a worried look.

"Slight jaundice to the eyes." The doctor had felt the sides of Sam's neck and then scribbled something else in the notes.

By the time he reached the ninth hole, the wind had picked up considerably. A dark blanket of cloud had rolled in off the ocean, plunging the golf course into a wintery twilight. He shivered. The hairs on his arm were standing on end.

"Good round?" Stan's head popped up above the counter in the office as he walked back through the door.

He shrugged his shoulders. "I've played better."

Stan got to his feet and walked round the desk. He looked behind him, no doubt to check that Mrs Murdoch wasn't within earshot. "Sorry about earlier. Maggie— she mean's well, but … you know."

He smiled and clasped Stan's outstretched hand. "She's a good woman, Stan. You treasure her."

Stan returned the smile. "We were both very sad to hear about Sam."

He didn't like the direction the conversation was taking at all. He let go of Stan's hand and swung his golf bag over his shoulder. "I must be going, Stan," he said,

164

regretting the curtness in his voice. He pressed his lips together into a smile. "Time waits for no man, and all that."

chapter eleven

SAM'S HANDS GRIPPED the armrests. The whole plane seemed to be vibrating with the bridled power of the two Rolls-Royce engines. Overhead the luggage bins creaked unnervingly. He half expected one of the compartments to drop open and dump its contents onto the heads of the passengers below. The creaking stopped the instant the captain released the brakes.

Three years in Otago and countless flights up and down the country had failed to cure Sam's inherent fear of flying. He opened his eyes to steal one last glimpse of the terminal building and then closed them tight as the plane lurched forward, down the runway.

To his relief, the journey was relatively uneventful, and as the plane ascended the east coast of the South Island, he even cracked open the blind to take a peek at the jagged line of mountains thousands of metres below. Stripped of snow, they looked barren and devoid of life.

During his first visit home, three years ago, he had asked after Tom. He had been unable to stop himself. When he discovered, through a friend of a friend, that Tom and his girlfriend had moved to Auckland, he had been both disappointed relieved. And from that point on, he had made a conscious effort to avoid the subject.

Towards the end of his first year at university, he had been offered an internship at a law firm in Christchurch. He had jumped at the chance. For three months that summer, he had lived with his grandparents and had cycled between his work in the city and their house at Sumner.

"We will shortly be commencing our descent into Wellington," the crackly voice of the purser echoed down the cabin. "Please return to your seats, fasten your seatbelts, and open your window blinds. Tray tables ..."

He had already stopped listening, mesmerised by the scenery below, his anxiety momentarily forgotten. From the air, the Marlborough Sounds were truly breathtaking—a winding maze of deep-blue channels, lush green isles, and turquoise bays.

He removed his headphones, wound the cord round his fingers several times and tucked it away in his pocket. His stomach muscles tensed as the plane banked for its final approach. A strong crosswind shook the cabin violently.

"Fucking hell," he cursed, gripping the armrests as they lost several metres in altitude. His knuckles turned white. He opened his eyes to find the elderly lady across the aisle glaring at him. "Sorry," he mumbled and looked away.

Holly was already waiting when they pulled into the drive. She was sitting on the front doorstep, arms clasped round her shins and her chin propped on her knees. Before the car had come to a stop, she was on her feet and striding across the grass towards him.

"Welcome home, stranger," she grinned, pulling him into a tight bear hug as he clambered out of the car. They had seen little of each other over the past three years, but whenever they were together, it was as if time had stood still. "Glad to be back?"

He smiled, but he didn't give Holly an answer. Over her shoulder, he could see the house. In some way, he had expected it to look different. He was slightly unnerved by how little had actually changed—from the blue and white agapanthus along the garden fence to the crack in the rendering beneath the kitchen window.

A car door slammed behind him. He turned just in time to see his mother disappear around the side of the house.

"She still hasn't forgiven me, then?" Holly asked, following him over to the car.

"Just ignore her," he replied. "I don't think she believes the bit in the Bible about forgiveness." He heaved his suitcase out of the boot. "I'll just take this inside and then we can go for a walk, eh?"

Holly followed him as far as the doorstep but stopped short of coming inside. When he re-emerged, she was rustling through a brown paper bag. "Want a lolly?"

"How are you not the size of a house already?" he laughed, slipping his hand into the bag and choosing a pineapple lump. His favourite.

Patch pulled on the lead all the way to the beach, and Sam was relieved when he was finally able to let him run free.

"So what's the deal with you and lover boy? It's Dan this time, isn't it?"

He shrugged. "We decided to call it a day," he replied absently. His eyes scanned the handful of surfers out on the water, but he didn't recognise any of them.

"How come?" Holly smoothed a patch of sand with one foot and then sat down, facing the ocean.

"It just didn't work out. We wanted to do different things," he said, dropping down beside her and clasping his arms round his shins.

He had met Dan at a bar in Dunedin. It had been fun for a couple of months, but it was over. He wasn't even sure where Dan was now.

"You'll never guess who I ran into the other day," Holly said, changing the subject.

Sam was watching Patch work his way methodically along the beach, sniffing each grain of sand. "Who?" he felt obliged to ask.

"That guy you went away with—that New Year before you left for university."

He turned and looked at her in disbelief. "Tom?"

"Yeah, that's the one. You know, I couldn't remember his name."

"Where?" His heart was racing now. He swallowed. All the moisture in his mouth seemed to have evaporated.

"At a party in Brooklyn," Holly answered casually. She traced a pattern in the sand and then scrubbed it out. "Are you OK?" she asked, looking up at him.

"Did you speak to him?" he asked, ignoring the question.

Holly chewed on her bottom lip. "For a bit."

"And what did you say?"

Holly looked as if she regretted having said anything.

169

"Just this and that," she replied.

"And did you tell him I was coming home?"

"I might have done."

He flopped back on the sand and looked up at the sky. So Tom was back. He could hear Holly rustling through her bag and snapped, "What are you looking for?"

"My smokes," she sighed, upending her bag into her lap and sorting through its contents. One by one, she flung keys, lipstick and several other unidentifiable objects back into the bag.

"Since when do you smoke?" he asked. He reached into his pocket and pulled out his own pack of cigarettes. He saw her shoulders relax at the sight of them.

"Since last year," she said, lighting the end of the cigarette and inhaling deeply. She tilted her head away from him as she exhaled.

"But you were always so against smoking."

Holly shrugged. "Yeah, well, that was before I'd ever had a university final."

He raised his eyebrows. "Well?"

"Well what?"

"What did he say to you?"

Holly flung the last of her belongings into her bag before she answered. "Did he ask after you, you mean?"

He averted his gaze. One of the surfers glided into his peripheral vision. "Well, did he?"

"Yeah, he did," Holly replied. Her face broke into a smile. Sam felt his heart double in size. "But his girlfriend was with him and she wasn't too happy about him talking to me." And then it imploded in on itself, like a dying star.

It took him almost a week to find out that Tom had moved back into the same flat.

"Why do you want to know?" Holly had asked.

"So that I can avoid running into him," he had replied. And he had meant it at the time. But the very next day he found himself climbing the familiar steps up to Tom's front door.

The front of the house had received a fresh coat of paint and the broken guttering had been repaired; but apart from that, nothing had changed. He gripped the hand rail and took a deep breath before knocking on the door.

"Hello." The girl he had seen with Tom all those years before answered the door. She looked slightly older, and her hairstyle was different, but he recognised her straight away.

"I—um—" his voice trailed off. He stood and stared, unable to think of what to say next.

"Can I help you?" she asked. The friendly expression on her face quickly changed to one of suspicion.

He shook his head and turned away. Her eyes followed him as he retreated down the steps and along the path.

It was spring before Sam had saved enough money to move out of his parents' house and into the city. He had found the advertisement one lunchbreak, pinned to the notice board at work.

"Catch!" his new flatmate, Neil, yelled, lobbing a can of beer across the room. He caught it and set it down on the coffee table to wait for the bubbles to settle.

Neil jumped over the back of the faded green sofa and

perched on one of the threadbare arms. "Not bad, eh, for twenty bucks!"

They had just lugged the sofa halfway across town and up two flights of stairs. His T-shirt was still damp with sweat and his arms were aching terribly.

"Yeah, not bad," he agreed, cracking open his beer. He had to clamp his mouth over the can to catch the foam that came bubbling up from inside.

"Shit, sorry, bro," Neil said, hopping to his feet and standing back to admire the new piece of furniture. "New" would be too generous. They had acquired it from the local second-hand store, and it had clearly seen better days.

"So are we going out tonight?" Neil asked.

He shifted uncomfortably in his seat and took another sip of his drink. For several weeks, he had managed to avoid going out drinking with Neil, but he was fast running out of excuses to stay home.

"I don't know if I can be bothered tonight," he said, avoiding Neil's eye. "I'm whacked from lugging all this stuff back to the flat." As well as a sofa, they had acquired a ring-marked coffee table and a bookcase with a missing shelf.

"Don't be a dick all your life, Sam," Neil replied. "I'm not going out on my own again. What about that sports bar on Courtenay Place?"

He shrugged. "What about it?"

"You're the local round here. What's it like? It seemed to be going off last night when I walked past. We'll start there, have a jug or two, and then move on in search of some ladies." He rubbed his palms together and grinned.

"I don't suppose you see too many of those on the farm, eh," Sam laughed, raising his right arm to deflect the cushion that came whizzing past his head. Born and raised in Taranaki, Neil had moved first to Auckland, for university, and then to Wellington for work.

"Yeah, it's OK, I guess. I haven't been there for years, though."

"Well then, it's time you reacquainted yourself." Neil finished off his beer and immediately opened another. "I'll teach you how to drink like we do on the farm."

Neil sat down next to him. He put his hand on his thighs and leaned forward, a serious expression on his face. "But before we do, I think there's something we need to talk about."

Sam felt his blood run cold. Nobody in Wellington knew he was gay, apart from Holly. He had gone to great lengths to keep it a secret while he was at university. Could it be that Neil had found out? New Zealand was frustratingly small at times.

"How easy are the girls in Wellington?" Neil asked.

He almost laughed with the relief. He shrugged his shoulders.

Neil seemed to accept the gesture as an adequate answer. "I guess we'll find out soon enough, eh," he said and ruffled Sam's hair as he stood up. "Another beer?"

He smiled and nodded. "Hey, when did you say that fridge was being delivered again?" They were still using a chilly bin topped up with ice from the dairy down the street.

"Next weekend, I think," Neil answered, handing him another can. "So you rooting anyone at the moment?"

He wanted to say, "Fuck off and mind your own business," but he shook his head. "Nah, not right now." For once he wasn't actually lying, he thought, with a tinge of irony.

"Me neither. It's been so long I think my balls are about to burst." Neil gripped his crotch and pretended to be weighing the contents of his hand. "Yep, pretty full."

"Eww," Sam grimaced. "Way too much information."

"Sharing is caring, Sammy," Neil said and gave him a friendly punch on the shoulder.

He was just about to take a sip from the can and managed to pour beer down his front instead. "Watch it, dick," he said.

It was close to ten when Neil appeared in the doorway. "You ready?"

Sam lifted up one side of his headphones. "Eh?"

"I said, are you ready to go?"

He couldn't help but stare at the amount of gel in Neil's hair—when he turned, it caught the light and made his scalp look like plastic.

He got up off the bed and reluctantly slipped on his shoes. "Are you planning on gassing the girls?" he asked, holding his nose and pretending to be overcome by the strength of Neil's aftershave.

"Oh, now there's an idea, Sammy," Neil grinned.

"Has anybody told you you're feral," he replied with a wry smile. "And stop calling me that already, will you? The name's Sam. Just Sam."

Out of the corner of his eye, he saw Neil pull a face.

It was pouring with rain as they made their way along Dixon Street, towards Courtenay Place. He kept as close

174

to the buildings as possible to avoid the spray from the tyres of the cars.

"Fuck, it's cold," Neil cursed.

He mumbled in agreement, pulling up the collar of his jacket and raising the zipper as far as it would go.

"IDs, lads," the doorman said as they walked up to the entrance of the sports bar on the corner. He reached into his back pocket and pulled out a dog-eared—and by now also rather damp—driver's licence. While the bouncer did the sums, he glanced at his feet and smiled. At least he had remembered to wear the right shoes this time.

"OK, boys. In you go." The doorman handed back their documents and stepped aside.

"I'll get the first round in!" he yelled over his shoulder, but Neil wasn't listening; his eyes were already scanning the room.

There were three staff serving at the bar but it seemed to take for ever to reach the front of the queue. As soon as he reached the front, he planted two elbows on the bar to secure his spot.

All three bar staff were men, but the one furthest away was especially cute. He watched out of the corner of his eye as the barman filled half a dozen shot glasses and handed them across the counter in pairs.

"What can I get you?" He wasn't paying attention and jumped when the barman shouted at him over the music. He pointed to the chiller cabinet and held up two fingers. "Two Heineken, please."

They had been there for no more than ten minutes and already Neil had managed to ingratiated himself with two girls. Sam had to admit he was impressed. Not the least because the girls appeared to be enjoying Neil's company.

"This is Erin," Neil nodded at the girl on his left, "And this is—"

"Julie," the other girl finished. "I'm Julie." She turned to him and held out her hand. He went to offer his own and then realised he was still holding both bottles of beer.

"Um," he mumbled, thrusting one of the bottles at Neil, "I'm Sam."

He smiled awkwardly as they shook hands. Thankfully, neither of the girls saw Neil nod at Julie and then wink at him.

"So, you're from Wellington?" he asked, paying Neil no attention.

"Yeah—Johnsonville," Erin answered.

Judging by the colour of Julie's cheeks, she felt as uncomfortable as he did. She nodded in agreement and sipped on her drink.

A long awkward silence ensued, during which he scanned the room in the hope of seeing a familiar face. He didn't usually find it difficult talking to girls; in many ways, it was much easier than talking to guys. But right now, he had never felt so uncomfortable.

"Do you come here often?" Erin asked. He almost laughed out loud but managed to stop himself.

"No," Neil replied for both of them. He then put an arm round Julie and whispered something in her ear. She giggled and her face flushed crimson.

"I haven't been here for years," he told Erin. "What about you?"

"A couple of times."

"Are you studying at Vic?" he asked. She looked a few years younger than he was—too old to be at college, too young to be at work. She nodded and proceeded to give him a full rundown of what she was studying. While she was talking, he allowed his eyes to wander.

Statistically, half a dozen guys in this room have to be gay, he surmised and set about trying to identify who the other five could be. One guy stood out immediately. He was standing among a group of girls on the other side of the dancefloor. Everything about him, from his clothes to the way he was standing, screamed "gay".

He glanced over at the bar. There was a lull in the queue, and the cute barman was chatting enthusiastically with a guy on the other side of the counter. He sized them up for a moment and decided that they were just friends.

"Are you OK?" Erin asked. She had stopped mid-sentence and was watching him. She must have seen all the blood drain from his face.

"Yeah," he mumbled in reply. "I—"

He craned his neck to get a better look across the room, but there was a group of people standing in the way.

"I thought I saw somebody I knew." He tried his best to sound casual, but his heart was racing. He turned to say something to Neil, and was annoyed to find that they had disappeared, leaving him alone with Erin.

Fuck!

He took a deep breath and forced out a smile. "Do you want another—"

He was going to say "drink?", but at the exact same moment, the crowd shifted again. He gulped.

On the other side of room, surrounded by friends, stood Tom. And he looked every bit as good as he had the last time they had seen each other, three years earlier. *No*, he corrected himself, *he looks better*.

"Are you sure you're OK?" Erin asked. She turned and looked in the same direction.

He felt light-headed. Feelings that he thought he had dealt with long ago began to resurface straightaway. It was as if time had stood still. He didn't know whether to laugh or cry.

He gasped for breath. His chest was tight. An invisible hand seemed to be squeezing his heart.

"I think we should find the others," Erin said, looking around for help.

He was still staring at Tom when Tom turned and looked in his direction. It took a few seconds for Tom's brain to process what he was seeing. When it did, his eyes almost doubled in size.

Sam smiled and nodded. He could feel a vein throbbing in his temple.

Before he could do anything, the crowd shifted again and the girl from Tom's flat appeared at Tom's side. She put her arm round Tom's waist and rested her head on his shoulder. She was laughing at something and was oblivious to the look of horror on Tom's face.

"What's the matter?" Neil reappeared, and he didn't look happy. The girls were standing to one side, whispering to each other. Neil leaned in close to him. "What's the deal, bro?" He motioned behind him. "Don't screw this up, eh."

He opened his mouth to reply but no words came out.

Everybody was watching him, waiting.

"I—" he started but didn't get any further. What could he say? "I—I don't feel well," he lied.

Neil looked distraught. "Wait here. I'll get you some water—"

"No," he cut him off. He was already backing away. If looks could kill, he would have been dead already. "I'm sorry," he mumbled again, pulling at the collar of his shirt, which suddenly felt several sizes too small. "I need to leave."

"Sam," Neil shouted after him but he kept walking.

He was soaked to the skin within minutes but he walked on regardless, numb, rivulets of ice-cold water streaming down his face and neck. His shirt clung to his frozen body. His skin was the same colour as the white cotton.

Right now, all he could think about was putting one foot in front of the other.

Neil had rung his cellphone immediately, but he had let it ring through to voicemail.

He stopped at Frank Kitts Park and sat down on one of the empty benches that faced out across the harbour. Opposite, the illuminated red-brick monastery of Saint Gerard towered over the bay below. It all looked so peaceful.

Slowly, the fog in his head began to clear.

What have I done? He pounded his forehead with the heel of his right hand. *What the fuck am I going to do now?*

When he awoke the next morning, it was still dark. In the few hours that he had been asleep, the top sheet had managed to wrap itself around his body like a cocoon.

He could hardly move. He pulled at the sheet to free himself, screwed it into a ball, and tossed it on the floor. It was almost as cold inside as it was outside, and each time he exhaled, his breath misted above his head.

He hauled himself to his feet and wandered down the hall towards the living room, the merino blanket his mother had given him the previous Christmas draped around his shoulders.

The door to Neil's room was open and his bed was empty. Clearly, he hadn't ruined Neil's prospects after all. The relief he felt was short-lived, though. As soon as he thought of Tom, his stomach cramped up again.

Watching television didn't prove as much of a distraction as he had hoped. Before long, he had exhausted the limited selection of channels and was back where he started.

He walked over to the window and pulled back the curtains. It was beginning to get light. The rooftops opposite stood out against the pale grey sky. He wiped away a patch of condensation and peered down at the street below.

Just a few hours before, the city had been a hive of activity, but now it was completely deserted. For a moment, he watched a flock of seagulls as they fought over what looked, at best, like the remnants of a kebab. He drew the curtains with a shudder of disgust.

It was a cold, crisp morning and he kept his hands in his pockets as he walked along the footpath, towards the bus stop.

To his relief, he didn't have to wait long; within a few minutes, the number six bus turned the corner and stopped several metres short of where he was standing. There was only one other person waiting—an elderly gentleman sitting quietly in the shelter behind him. He stood to one side to let him by.

"Two zones, please," he said, handing over the exact fare. The driver didn't even look up. A paper slip popped out the side of the ticket machine, and he tore it off along the serrated edge.

He had taken, at most, half a dozen steps when the bus lurched forward. His feet shot out from under him and he flew down the aisle, colliding with one of the upright posts and almost landing in the lap of a young woman who was gazing out the window.

"Sorry," he said, dropping onto the seat behind her. He looked up to find several smiling faces.

He wasn't at all sure he was doing the right thing, but he had to speak to Tom. He knew that he wouldn't be able to function like a normal human being until he had. With a sigh, he rested his head against the misted glass windowpane. The vibration of the bus made his teeth rattle.

"Oh God," he groaned as he realised for the first time that Tom's girlfriend answer the door.

He thought about getting off at the next stop and walking back to the flat, but something kept him in his seat. He rang the bell and got off at the first stop on the Hataitai side of the bus tunnel. Tom's flat was a few minutes' walk from the dairy on the corner of Moxham Avenue and Waitoa Road.

The street was completely still, and the wooden steps up to Tom's flat were deep in the shadows. He held his breath as he put his full weight on the first step. To his relief, it didn't betray his presence.

Somewhere overhead, a seagull squawked in protest, but he continued, the need to see Tom carrying him the final few metres.

It was almost impossible to see through the frosted pane in the door. He had to cup his hands over his eyes and push his nose right up against the glass. *Hopefully, none of the neighbours is watching.* From the street, it probably looked as if he was casing the joint.

He held his breath and listened carefully, but he couldn't hear anything over the thump of his own heart. Within, the flat was silent.

Of course, they're all asleep, he berated himself. He felt like a fool. *You're the only moron awake at this time.*

He rubbed a hand across the nape of his neck as he tried to assess his options. He could ring the doorbell and wake Tom—and the rest of the flat. If he did, he would almost certainly have some explaining to do.

Again he pictured Tom's girlfriend answering the door. He shuddered at the thought.

Instead of heading back the way he had come, he continued down Moxham Avenue, towards Kilbirnie and the beach beyond. But as he reached the church on the corner, Tom came flying round the bend, barreling straight towards him. He barely had time to jump out of the way.

Tom stopped a few metres further along the footpath. He leaned forward on his knees, gasping for breath. His bright-red T-shirt was maroon beneath the arms and all down his back. Tom shook the hair out of his eyes and looked up.

"Sam." Tom spat in the gutter as he straightened up. "What are you going here?"

"What are you doing here?"

He felt himself bristle, but before he was able to answer, he heard footsteps behind him. He turned to find Tom's girlfriend walking towards them.

He had no intention of waiting to see whether she remembered him. He glanced once at Tom and then ran in the opposite direction.

"You look like shit." Holly peered at him over the rim of her extra-shot, trim latte. She had never been one to pull any punches. "What the hell happened to you?"

The terrace of the café was packed. He slipped onto the seat Holly had saved for him.

"Sorry I'm late," he said, picking up the menu and scanning the list of hot drinks.

"So?" Holly raised her eyebrows. "Why the amateur dramatics on the telephone?"

Thankfully, a waitress appeared at that very moment.

"It's Tom," he said, once the waitress was out of earshot.

"I worked that much out." Holly took a deep breath, as if she was preparing to deal with a difficult child. "So are you going to tell me what's going on?"

He leaned back and gazed up into the vast expanse of blue above. Overnight the wind had changed. Now it was blowing from the north again. He would never work the Wellington weather out. One day, it could be the dead of winter; the next, people would be walking round in shorts and T-shirts. "Do we have to talk about it just now?"

"Hell, yeah." Holly crossed her arms. "That's what happens when you wake me up at the crack of dawn, *and* on a weekend!"

"It wasn't the crack of dawn; it was past nine," he protested.

Holly didn't say anything; she simply raised her eyebrows and gave him one of her looks.

"OK, OK," he gave in. "I saw him in town last night. I didn't plan to; it just happened."

"What happened?" she asked, taking another sip of her coffee.

"Well—nothing really," he was forced to admit.

"Did you kiss?"

"Sshh," he hissed, "not so loud, eh?"

Holly raised her eyebrows, as if to say, "Go on."

"No, we didn't." While he spoke, he focused on a spot on the horizon just above Holly's right shoulder.

"You did talk to him, though?"

He could feel his face turning crimson. He didn't reply.

"You didn't even talk to him?" Holly asked. She didn't bother to mask her disbelief.

He shook his head.

"So what's all the fuss about?"

He gave her a dark look. He loved Holly—ever since sex had been taken off the table, she had been one of his staunchest friends—but sometimes she could be so fucking insensitive.

The waitress arrived with his flat white and they sat in silence until she had gone again.

"Sorry, I'm just surprised—that's all. I thought you were going to tell me you'd gone home with him."

Her voice was like a foghorn, and he squirmed in his seat, but nobody was paying them any attention.

Holly lifted her handbag off the floor, placed it in front of her, and started to rummage through its contents.

"Ah ha, found you!" She withdrew a pink, plastic lipstick and applied a fresh coat.

"What do I do, Hols?"

She exhaled loudly and tossed her lipstick back into her handbag. "Do?"

"Yes, what do I do?"

A stone's throw from the café, the little ferry that crisscrossed the harbour every day was coming into dock. Its engines laboured in reverse as the skipper edged the boat up against the steel pontoon and lowered the gangplank with a crash. The noise seemed to cleave his brain in two.

"You don't do anything," Holly said.

He sighed and slumped in the chair. He didn't know why he had asked for Holly's opinion. He knew that would be her answer.

"He had a girl with him last night."

Holly sat up straight, her interest piqued.

"So I went over to his flat this morning. I didn't really have a choice—I had to talk to him."

"And?"

"He wasn't there," he said. "I mean, he was, but he was out running. He arrived back just as I was leaving."

"And did you speak to him then?" He shook his head.

"For fuck's sake, why not?"

"She was with him again."

"Who—oh. Well, so?"

He almost choked on his coffee. "What do you mean 'so?'?"

"Well, it's just a hello, not a declaration of eternal love."

He shifted awkwardly on his chair. "She might have remembered me."

Holly raised her eyebrows again.

"I didn't tell you, but a few months ago I went round to the flat."

Holly sighed.

"She answered the door—the same girl." He took a deep breath before continuing, "And I ran away."

"I see," Holly answered. "And have you told Neil yet?" she asked, changing the subject.

"I haven't found the right time," he answered, defensively.

"You *do* know that the longer you leave it, the harder it's going to get, don't you?"

This time it was he who raised his eyebrows.

"OK, OK, stupid question."

"Do you believe in God?" he asked.

Holly paused, her cup halfway to her lips. Without taking a sip, she put the cup back on the table and took a deep breath. "I don't know. Do you?"

"I'm not sure," he answered honestly. "I mean, I used to. At least I think I did. I never knew any different. But I don't know what I believe in any more."

"And does it matter?" she asked, draining her cup and running a finger round the inside to scoop up the last of the froth.

"It matters to my mum," he replied. "She believes in God completely. It drives my dad crazy, but he's grown

186

to accept it—anything for an easy life, I guess. And it keeps her nice and submissive, so I guess it's got its benefits."

He breathed in through his nose and shook his head.

"I sort of envy her in a way, you know?"

Holly looked slightly confused, so he tried to explain another way.

"She has no doubts—or none that she will ever admit to. She knows what she believes, and so she's happy. Even if it means taking a few knocks every now and then. And she doesn't care what anybody thinks of her."

"And neither should you!" Holly fired back. "Who cares if you're gay?"

An American couple at the next table looked up from their guidebook to the South Island and cast him a wary glance.

"You don't get it. My mum doesn't believe in being—" He lowered his voice before he continued. "She doesn't believe in being gay. She'll flip if she finds out. And if I tell Neil, she might very well find out. I can't take the risk—not at the moment."

He stopped talking and stared vacantly into his own empty cup.

Holly stood up and put on her coat. "Come up to uni with me. I've got some books to collect for my assignment that was due last week." She sighed. "I wish I'd never started this stupid master's."

chapter twelve

THE FOLLOWING FRIDAY, Sam went straight from the office to his parents' house, where he stayed for most of the evening. When the clock in the hall struck half past ten, he finally got to his feet. If Neil hadn't gone out for the night already, he would be shortly. With any luck, he would be gone by the time he arrived home.

"Are you off?" his mother asked. She folded down the corner of her book so that she didn't lose her place.

"Yeah, Mum. I think I'll head back to the flat now," he replied, stretching. He leaned down and gave her a kiss on the cheek. "Thanks for tea."

He didn't like leaving his mother alone when his father was out drinking. It was impossible to predict the mood he would be in when he eventually came home.

"Just be careful, Sam," she said, following him out into the hall. "Go straight home and call me as soon as you get there."

He put his arms round her and gave her a bear hug. She smelled like Mum. He breathed in deeply, committing her scent to memory.

He got off the bus at Kent Terrace and made his way

home via the backstreets, bypassing the crowded bars on Courtenay Place and the risk of running into Neil or Tom.

It had been drizzling off and on all afternoon, but the rain was getting stronger now. He squirmed as a large, cold droplet ran down his neck, between his shoulder blades. He pulled his collar up as far as it would go and quickened his pace. The first clap of thunder sounded just as he reached the front door to the flat.

When he saw that all the lights were turned off, he breathed a sigh of relief.

The recent damp weather had expanded the wooden doorframe, making it almost impossible to enter the flat quietly. He slid the key into the lock and shoved the door hard with his shoulder. It didn't budge on the first attempt, but on the second it gave way and he almost fell headfirst into the hall.

"Fucking door," he cursed, yanking the key out of the lock and wiping the water from his brow with his forearm.

He was just about to slam the door shut when he heard a voice call his name.

"Sam!"

He turned to see Tom step out of the shadow of a doorway across the street.

"I've been out," he blurted in reply.

The corner of Tom's mouth turned up ever so slightly. "I know."

He felt his stomach contract into a tight ball.

"Come for a drink." Tom stepped into the light of the nearest streetlamp. "Please. We need to talk."

He took a deep breath and tried to think of what to say, and do, next.

"Won't your girlfriend mind?" He hadn't meant to sound so aggressive, and when Tom winced, he regretted what he had said.

"She's up the coast with her parents this weekend."

Instantly, he felt his hackles rise. Hearing Tom speak of her so freely cut like a knife. He hadn't realised it was possible to seethe with jealousy.

"Oh, I see," he said. This time the tone of his voice was intentional, and he felt no remorse.

"Please," Tom repeated. "One drink and then I'll leave."

Without saying a word, he stepped out onto the footpath and yanked the door shut behind him.

Wherever Tom went, heads turned, and as they walked into the pub, a group of girls sitting at a table near the door looked up. He pretended not to notice and followed Tom into the crowd.

There was a band playing on the stage at the far end of the bar, making it was almost impossible to hold a conversation.

"Shall we go outside?" Tom shouted over the music. He passed him a handle of beer and motioned towards the small smoking area outside.

The garden bar had a small awning, but given the atrocious weather, it was almost entirely deserted.

They drank in silence for a while. Just when he was beginning to think they might never talk, Tom set his glass down and looked up.

"I'm sorry about the other night," Tom said. His Adam's apple twitched as he swallowed.

The fresh air and beer had gone a small way to calming

Sam's temper. "Don't worry about it," he replied, draining the last of his beer and getting to his feet. "Want another?"

"Yeah, cheers."

Now that the ice had been broken, the conversation flowed more easily.

"So are you back for good?" Tom asked as soon as he returned. "Cheers, by the way," he added, raising his glass.

"Cheers," Sam replied and they chinked glasses. "I guess so." He fumbled in his pocket for his cigarettes.

"Want one?" He offered the pack to Tom, who shook his head. He suddenly felt self-conscious and returned the packet to his pocket unopened. "I've been back a couple of months now but I've only been living in the city a couple of weeks."

"Are you living alone?"

He shook his head. "No, with a guy from work. He's nice enough."

Tom looked as if he wanted to ask something, but he kept his mouth closed.

"Anyway, enough about me," Sam said, prompting Tom to speak. "What's new with you? Still living in the same flat, I see."

He didn't mention that Holly had already filled him in on the details.

"Yeah," Tom replied, shifting in his seat. If Tom's plan had been to kill the mood, he succeeded the instant he mentioned his girlfriend. "You know that Eve lives there now too."

He felt the muscles in his face harden. "I saw."

Tom must have heard the change in his voice. He looked up and their eyes met. "She's nice, you know. You'd like her."

"Why are you telling me this?"

If Tom thought he was going to sit here and listen to how great Eve was, he could whistle. He pushed back his chair and stood to leave but Tom reached across the table and gripped his forearm. "Don't go."

He froze. All his senses converged on Tom's hand.

"Sorry." Tom released his grip. "Please stay. Just a bit longer."

He sat down. His skin tingled where Tom's hand had been. "Why are you here?" he asked.

Tom contemplated the question before taking a deep breath and saying, "I don't know."

The music stopped and the band left the stage.

"Let's go inside, eh? It's emptied out a bit now."

Tom looked at his watch. "I should really be going," he replied, but he made no move to leave.

"Come back to mine if you want?" The words were out of Sam's mouth before he realised what he was saying.

Tom's eyes widened. He looked like a rabbit caught in the headlights.

"For a drink. That's all."

When he opened the door to the flat, he was relieved to find the lights were still turned off. On the walk home from the bar, he had been worried that Neil might have come home early.

"What do you want to drink? We haven't got much except beer."

"A beer would be great, thanks," Tom said, his eyes

192

roaming round the room. He walked over to the window and looked out. "It's a pretty awesome spot you've got here."

He handed Tom a can. "Thanks."

Tom cracked the tab and the gas that was trapped inside escaped with a hiss. He took a sip. "Don't you keep your beers in the fridge?" he said, screwing up his face.

Sam motioned to the chilly bin sitting on the kitchen bench. "Not yet, we don't."

"Oh—right." Tom glanced out of the window again. His cheeks were slightly flushed.

There was a long, awkward silence before they both spoke at once.

"I'm sorry—"

"So does—"

Tom turned and smiled.

"You go first," Sam said.

"Does—what's your flatmate called, again?"

"Neil."

"Are you and Neil—" Tom began to ask, but Sam shook his head before he could finish the question. "Does Neil know?" Tom asked instead.

He looked Tom in the eye as he took a swig from his can. "Know what?"

Tom didn't answer the question.

The alcohol had been at work without his realising it, stripping away his inhibitions. Now, for the first time, he realised that the knot in his stomach was gone.

He took a step closer to Tom.

"Does—what's your girlfriend's name again?" he

asked. Eve's name would be seared in his memory for ever, but he wasn't about to let Tom know that.

Tom's head jerked up. "Eve," he replied. He sounded wary.

"Does she know?"

He saw Tom's body stiffen. Anger flashed across his face. "Sam, I'm not—"

With a boldness he never knew he possessed, he stepped forward and silenced Tom with a kiss.

For a moment, neither of them moved. They stood completely still—two statues joined by the lips.

"I'm sorry," he said, breaking away at last.

This time, it was Tom who took the lead. Tom grabbed his arm and pulled him towards him. Before he knew what was happening, they were kissing again.

"I—"

"Don't speak, eh?" Tom whispered in his ear. He could barely hear him over the pounding of his heart. "Take me to your room," Tom said.

Tom's body pushed against his as they kissed. An unmistakable hardness pressed into his stomach.

His own boxer shorts were getting wetter by the second. If he didn't slow things down, it would all be over within seconds. As if sensing his thoughts, Tom leaned back and smiled.

A mischievous grin on his face, Tom ran a hand along the inside of Sam's thigh and up the leg of his boxer shorts. Sam groaned and arched his back. Tom leaned down and kissed him again.

With his hands, Sam traced the contours of Tom's body. He really was all muscle. He ran his fingers along

194

Tom's spine and cupped a buttock.

The next thing he knew, they were both naked, their chests almost touching. Tom thrust his hips against him, slowly at first, then with increasing urgency, and he had to bite down on Tom's shoulder to stop from crying out. Trickles of sweat ran down Tom's nose and dropped into his eyes, but he blinked them away.

As he came, his whole body convulsed, pulling Tom over the edge with him.

Tom slumped forward and rested his forehead on his shoulder. He could feel the warmth of Tom's breath, quick and shallow, against his neck.

With one, sharp inhalation of breath, Tom rolled off of him.

Tom lay on his side, put an arm round his middle, and pulled him close, so that his buttocks were nestled in the curve of Tom's stomach.

For a long while they lay in silence. "'Night," he whispered at last. But Tom didn't reply; he was already fast asleep.

Tom was awake when he opened his eyes.

"'Morning." Tom rolled onto his side to face him. The curtains were open, and in the morning light, his eyes looked like bottomless pools.

"'Morning," he said. He knew he was grinning like an idiot but he couldn't help himself. He reached out a hand and touched the side of Tom's face, just to reassure himself that he wasn't dreaming.

He traced the line of Tom's jaw. His skin was coarse, like sandpaper. When his fingers reached Tom's mouth, Tom snapped his teeth playfully.

"I should be going," Tom said, resting his forehead against his.

"Already?"

Tom didn't reply. He threw back the covers, and the sudden inrush of cold air made them both shiver.

"Cold, eh," Tom said, jumping out of bed and making a grab for his clothes. His naked body was even more magnificent in the daylight. When Tom turned round, he caught a glimpse of Tom's cock in all its glory.

"When will I see you again?" he asked, trying not to stare.

Tom walked over to the bed and stood beside it. The window was open and the curtains inflated like sails behind him. But just as Tom opened his mouth to speak, the bedroom door opened.

"Bro, can I borrow—" Neil froze in the doorway, his mouth wide open. His eyes went first to Tom, then to the bed. When Neil's eyes registered the extra depression in the mattress, they grew large as saucers.

"Fuck," Sam cursed. He flew out of the bed towards Neil. "Haven't you heard of knocking?"

Neil mumbled an apology as he was ejected from the room.

He shut the door in Neil's face.

"Don't go" was the first, and only, thing he could think to say. He took a step towards Tom, but Tom recoiled. "I'll talk to him," he said. "Please don't leave."

The panic in his voice was palpable. He could feel tears welling in his eyes, but he was determined not to cry. He took a deep breath. "Can I see you later?"

Tom opened his mouth to speak and then closed it again without saying a word.

They stood in silence for a moment. Outside, in the street, there was a shriek of laughter. The sound cut like a knife.

"I can't do this," Tom said at last, avoiding his eye. He took a step towards the door. "I've got to go."

He couldn't—wouldn't—watch Tom leave. He walked over to the window and looked out. Overhead, a seagull squawked. He watched, blurry eyed, as the gull swooped down and plucked something out of the gutter.

The whole flat shook as the front door slammed. A solitary tear broke free, as if dislodged by the impact, and ran down his cheek.

"HE HASN'T LEFT his room in days. What should I do?"

He turned his ear towards the crack in the door. Neil was standing at the end of the hall with his back to him. He was holding the telephone in one hand and was playing nervously with the cord with the other.

As soon as Neil hung up the phone, he shot back into bed and pulled the covers over his head.

He really needed to pee. If Neil didn't go out soon, he would have to make a dash for the bathroom and hope he didn't notice.

Why can't they just leave me alone? he thought.

Talking about things wasn't always best. There were times when bottling them up and pretending they had never happened was a far better solution.

It was midday when Holly arrived. She banged several times on his bedroom door. "I know you can hear me, Sam!" she shouted. And then, when he still hadn't responded, "I'm coming in."

Holly walked over to the window and threw open the curtains. The brightness of the sunlight threw his surroundings into stark relief. His room was an absolute mess.

"You've got to snap out of this," she said.

He felt the mattress dip as she sat on the edge of the bed. She gave his shoulder a shake, but he groaned and shrugged it off.

"You know, when my dad left, my mum didn't get out of bed for a week. At the end of that week her bedroom didn't smell too good. To tell you the truth, it smells worse in here."

"Go away," he murmured from beneath the covers.

"There are plenty more fish in the sea, Sam," she continued, undeterred. "OK, maybe not in Wellington admittedly, but there's always Sydney. I hear the scene is pretty epic over there. One of the girls at Vic went there last year and she said Oxford Street was amazing."

He was fighting a losing battle. He rolled onto his back and propped himself up on his elbows. "What do you want, Holly?"

"To check you're OK, of course," she replied, ruffling his already messed up hair.

He forced out a smile. "I'm fine. Really. I just want to be on my own right now."

Holly stood and walked out of the room. Perhaps she had actually listened? There was a first for everything. But, to his horror, she returned several minutes later, a browbeaten Neil in tow.

Neil stood just inside the doorway and scuffed at the carpet until Holly ordered him into the room.

"Go on," she glared and then nodded in his direction.

Neil had a pained expression on his face, but, clearly, he had his instructions. As Neil spoke, his eyes seemed to focus on a spot to the left of Sam's face. "It's OK if you want to be gay, bro."

Holly glared again and Neil promptly changed tack.

"Sorry—what I meant to say was: it's OK with me."

Holly had had enough now and jumped in. "What he's trying to say"—she looked at Neil and shook her head—"is that you don't have to hide away in your room. We're here for you."

He glanced in Neil's direction, and for a second they made eye contact. Neil smiled and nodded his head.

"Get up and come for a coffee," Holly continued. "It'll do you good to get some fresh air. You can't stay in here for ever."

Out the corner of his eye, he saw Neil slip away while she wasn't looking, and he almost smiled.

"I think I'll just stay here a bit longer," he replied. He yawned for effect and held a hand in front of his mouth.

Holly gave him a long, penetrating look, as if she were sizing up this particular battle. Then she sighed and got to her feet. "Just promise you won't do anything stupid."

He nodded.

"OK, then. I'll be back tomorrow. And you'll be leaving this room—so be warned."

He dreamt that he was fighting with Tom. But Tom's face kept changing. One moment, he was staring straight into Tom's blue eyes; the next, he was face to face with his mother. "You're going to hell!" she screamed like a

199

banshee. And then, in another breath, she was gone, and he was back in the flat, alone with Neil.

He was disoriented when he woke. Somewhere a bell was ringing. Yet it seemed to have a ghostly quality. It took him a few moments to realise that the noise wasn't a part of his dream—that it was coming from the hallway.

"Doorbell," he thought groggily. Perhaps if he ignored it, whomever it was would go away.

Right on cue, the ringing stopped.

He breathed a sigh of relief, savouring the renewed silence. Every muscle, every joint in his body ached. He felt as if he had gone ten rounds in the ring.

The peace was short-lived.

"Fuck off!" he yelled when the ringing started up again. But this time, it didn't stop.

He dragged himself out of bed and trudged down the hall to the intercom. He didn't bother to ask who it was before he buzzed them in.

He stood on the doorstep, his arms folded protectively in front of his body. It was cold and he was wearing only track pants and a T-shirt. The sound of the rain lashing wildly against the windows in the living room made him shiver.

First he heard footsteps on the staircase. Then the back of a blond head came into view. Tom's head. He froze.

Tom was soaking wet. He looked as if he had just taken a shower with all his clothes on. When he rounded the last turn in the stairs, they came face to face.

"Hi." Tom pressed his lips together and brushed a lock of hair away from his eyes. He looked nervous.

Sam didn't reply. He was stunned. Part of him wanted

to run to Tom; the other wanted to slam the door in his face.

Tom must have sensed his indecision. He took a step forward and then stopped. He looked down at the floor as he spoke. "Can I come in?"

Clearly, Tom hadn't been expecting it to rain. He hadn't brought a jacket with him, and the fitted shirt that he was wearing clung to his body. His nipples were protruding through the wet cotton.

"Please," Tom said, "I really need to talk to you."

The instant that Tom smiled, Sam felt the last vestiges of his anger melt away. He stepped aside without saying a word.

"Here." He passed Tom a clean towel out of the hot-water cupboard and waited in silence as he dried his arms, neck and face.

"I couldn't borrow some clothes, could I?" Tom asked. He was still shivering uncontrollably, and his skin had turned a slightly concerning shade of blue.

While he was searching through the wardrobe, Tom stripped down to his undies and hung his wet clothes over the back of a chair. He tied the towel low round his waist.

Sam tried not to look, but the temptation was too great.

"Give those to me," he said, taking Tom's wet jeans and exchanging them for a dry pair. "I'll put them in the dryer."

As he turned to walk away, Tom reached out and touched his shoulder. "I broke up with Eve."

He stopped dead. Slowly he turned round to face Tom. "Say what?"

A grin spread across Tom's face. "I broke up with Eve," he repeated.

He stared at Tom, uncomprehending. It sounded as if Tom had ended things with his girlfriend.

"I. Broke. Up. With. Eve."

"I—"

He was at a complete loss for words. Endorphins were flooding his brain, muddling all his senses. "I don't understand," he sighed. "Why?"

He hadn't meant to be quite so blunt, but he was still reeling under the shock of what he had just heard.

"*Why?*" Tom repeated, his smile vanishing. He looked crestfallen.

Sam lowered his eyes to the floor.

Tom closed the gap between them. Tom was shaking too now.

"Because of you," Tom said, his voice almost a whisper. Tom placed a hand under his chin and forced him to lift his head. Then he leaned in so that their lips were almost touching. He could feel the warmth of Tom's breath on his face each time he exhaled.

"I want you."

He gulped and closed his eyes.

The whole world melted away when Tom kissed him.

They were standing in the kitchen when Sam heard the key turn in the lock. Tom was right behind him, his arms wrapped round his waist. He managed to disentangle himself just as Neil wandered into the room.

Neil was playing with his phone and didn't notice, but as he looked up and saw Tom, he froze in his tracks.

"Sorry," Neil murmured, backing away as if he had

just stumbled upon a wild animal.

"Fuck," Sam cursed once they were alone again. He ran a hand through his hair and squeezed the back of his neck. "Fuck."

Without saying a word, Tom disappeared into the laundry. When he returned a few minutes later, he was wearing his own things.

Sam felt his stomach drop through the floor. He had no desire, or strength, to hear what Tom was about to say.

When Tom smiled and said, "Talk later, then," he nearly laughed with relief.

He nodded, momentarily incapable of speech.

With a quick glance over his shoulder, Tom stepped forward and planted a kiss on his lips.

chapter thirteen

Sam's grandparents telephoned as they were driving off the ferry. They were heading north, caravan in tow, and had chosen to break their journey in Wellington.

"Tell him to wait at the end of the street," he could hear his grandfather barking in the background. He didn't sound happy.

His mother was cooking a meal in their honour and had given them strict instructions to collect him on their way through the city.

"Wait at the end of the street, dear," his grandmother repeated. "We won't be long." There was a brief pause and then, "Now, how do you hang up this blasted—" as she cut herself off.

He smiled as he returned the phone to its cradle. He was in an exceptionally good mood today. Even his grandfather's bad-temperedness couldn't bring him down.

The instant they walked through the door, it was obvious that something was wrong.

"What's the matter?" he asked, slowly taking off his coat and draping it over the back of a dining chair. He couldn't smell any food. Instead of preparing the lunch, his mother was sitting on the sofa. She had her face in her hands.

His grandparents appeared behind him. They were still fussing with their things, oblivious to the tension in the room.

He looked around for his sister but she was nowhere to be seen. "Where's Catherine?" he asked, a stab of fear in his gut. Had something happened to her?

"She's at your aunt's house," his father grunted. He turned around. He hadn't noticed his father standing over by the window.

"But Gran and Grandad are here," he replied. What his father had said made no sense.

His father cleared his throat to speak. "Sam, sit down."

His blood ran cold in his veins.

"Where's Catherine?" his grandmother interrupted, stepping round him, into the room, but his father simply ignored the question. She turned to her daughter instead. "Susan, where is Catherine?"

"She's fine, Mum."

When his mother raised her head, he saw that she had been crying.

"Something disturbing has been brought to our attention," his father continued.

He gulped back the impulse to vomit.

His grandmother looked at his father and then turned to him. "Sam, what's going on?"

"Stay out of it, Jean," his father snapped. His grandmother bristled but she kept her mouth closed. "Sam—sit," his father repeated.

He did as he was told, almost collapsing onto the nearest chair. He closed his eyes and waited for the axe to fall.

"What on earth is going on here?" his grandfather said, walking into the room at last.

"Yes, will somebody *please* tell us what's going on?" his grandmother echoed.

His father's voice cut straight through the fog in his head. "People are saying things about you, Sam."

He swallowed. His head was swimming. He couldn't have replied even if he had wanted to.

There was no time to react when his father lunged forward and grabbed him by the arm. His father squeezed so hard that he had to bite down on his bottom lip not to cry out.

"Why are they saying these things?" his father said, shaking his arm. "Why, Sam?"

For the first time, he saw fear in his father's eyes.

Suddenly, an incredible weariness descended on him and he sighed. He was tired of telling lies. It was exhausting, living a life that wasn't real—making up stories and trying to remember what he had said and whom he had said it to.

He took a deep breath, fixed his thoughts on Tom, and said, "It's true."

A few seconds passed without anything happening. But then his father's face hardened. Behind him, he heard his mother break into renewed sobs.

His father flung his arm away and stood up straight. All the blood had rushed back into his face. "Get out of this house."

He didn't move, though. He was too stunned. Had he really just said what he thought he had said? It hadn't been nearly as difficult as he had been expecting. He almost laughed, but managed to stop himself.

His grandmother looked at them each in turn. "Will somebody please tell me what is going on here?" she demanded. By the tone of her voice, it was clear she wouldn't be fobbed off again.

"Your grandson," his father pointed at him but didn't make eye contact, "is a dirty little pervert. Is that what you want to hear?"

His grandmother turned her back on her son-in-law and asked, "What is your lunatic of a father talking about?"

The sense of relief he had felt only moments before was gone. His breath was coming short and shallow now. He couldn't get the air into his lungs fast enough.

"Sam," his grandmother said. She took a step towards him, but his father reached him first.

"I thought I told you to leave this house!" his father thundered, grabbing hold of him again and pulling him out of his seat. He was too dazed to put up a fight.

His grandmother tried to wedge herself between them, but his father pushed her aside as if she didn't weigh a thing.

When they reached the doorstep, he tripped and stumbled headfirst into the yard, landing on his hands and knees. The jagged surface of the drive sliced through his palms like a hot knife through butter.

His grandmother was by his side in a flash. She cradled him against her body, paying no attention to the blood that was running down his arms.

"I'm sorry," he mumbled, trying not to stain her white blouse. She rested her cheek against the top of his head and held him tight.

"Don't speak," she murmured in his ear.

But his father wasn't about to give up yet. "Go on, what are you waiting for? Sling your hook," he sneered, reaching for him again.

His grandmother held his father at arm's length. "Touch the boy again, and by God I swear you'll regret it," she hissed. Such was the ferocity in her voice that his father actually backed off.

"How could you do this to us?" his father said. He looked more distraught than angry now. "Do you realise what you've done? You've made us into a laughing stock."

"That's enough now, John."

His father turned to find his father-in-law standing directly behind him.

The older men stared at each other, neither blinking. The tension in the air was palpable, and for a moment he thought one might actually strike the other. It was exactly like watching two pack animals vie for top spot.

To his surprise, his father was the first to yield. He marched into the house and slammed the door behind him.

"Jean, go and find that daughter of ours and tell her to get out here immediately."

His grandmother released him, but before she let go completely, she cupped his face in her hands. "We love you. Nothing has changed."

He tried to smile through the tears that were streaming down his face.

"Go, Jean," his grandfather said gently, pulling her away. When she was gone, his grandfather sat down next to him.

"Sam, what your grandmother said is true." His grandfather put a hand on his shoulder and gave it a gentle squeeze. "But I won't pretend I'm not disappointed."

His grandfather must have felt his body tense.

"Hear me out, will you?"

He nodded.

"I'm disappointed because you have a tough road ahead of you. As you have just witnessed, the world is full of wankers."

His eyes widened; he had never heard his grandfather swear before.

"That's right," his grandfather chuckled. "But you will have our full support—OK?" His grandfather gave his shoulder another squeeze. "Now, get in the car. Your grandmother and I will take you out for tea."

WHEN TOM SUGGESTED that they get away for a few days—*just until the dust settles*—he didn't need to think twice. The doctor had already signed him off work for a week with stress.

"Great. I'll book us on the first ferry in the morning." Tom leaned in for a kiss before throwing back the covers and climbing out of the bed. Tom's boxer shorts had ridden down at the back, exposing the cleft of his buttocks.

He smiled as he pulled the duvet up round his chin and burrowed into the warm spot that Tom's body had made. The pillow smelled of Tom's aftershave and he inhaled deeply.

The next morning, they were up before dawn. Neil was still fast asleep when they called in at his flat to collect his things. For once, Neil's guttural snoring wasn't an unwelcome sound.

"I'll be as quick as I can," he whispered, leaving Tom at the door. He crept into his room and silently gathered together enough clothes to last for several days.

"Ready," he whispered, throwing the backpack over his shoulder and quietly closing the bedroom door behind him. On the way out, he left a note on the kitchen bench, telling Neil that he would be back in a few days.

It was a still morning and the deck barely moved as the ferry glided past the small island in the centre of the harbour, out towards the choppier waters of Cook Strait.

They climbed to the top deck and found a row of empty seats towards the stern, as far away from the other passengers as they could get. Despite the calm weather, Tom was already looking green.

The seats were covered with dew and the moisture seeped straight through the seat of his pants.

"Are you sure you're OK?" he asked. Tom grunted in reply but didn't look up from between his knees.

With every minute that passed, the sky grew lighter in the east. Before long the horizon came into focus. The navy blue of the sky contrasted with the blackness of the ocean below.

It was freezing cold. Each breath condensed into white mist.

With a quick glance to check that nobody was watching,

he put a hand on Tom's leg and gave it a squeeze. "Let's go inside, eh? It's freezing out here."

Tom nodded in agreement.

Just as they were getting to their feet, the ferry rounded the last headland. The bow rose sharply as it crested a wave and then pitched forward, the deck falling away beneath them. Tom made a dash for the railing. He reached it just in time and vomited over the side of the ship.

"Thank fuck we have wind behind us." Sam tried to lighten the mood, but Tom didn't respond. He hung limp over the railing.

"You go in," Tom groaned, turning his head and looking at him through tear-filled eyes. He wiped his mouth on his sleeve. "I'll stay out here for a bit longer."

They stayed up on deck for most of the crossing, even when they had reached the still waters of the Marlborough Sounds. Tom's face lost its green tinge only after they disembarked in Picton.

They picked up a hire car at the ferry terminal—a rusty old hatch that had seen better days.

"Where to, Miss Penelope?" Tom said with a grin. Clearly, he was feeling better. He spread the road map out over the steering wheel. "It's an hour or two to Nelson, and then a couple more to the Abel Tasman National Park, or we could head south, towards Kaikoura."

He leaned in to look at the map. "I don't mind," he said. So long as they were together, he would be happy.

Tom folded up the map and handed it to him. "Abel Tasman it is, then," he smiled.

They drove in silence for a while, past seemingly

endless rows of bare vines. In the distance, white-capped mountains rose up out of the earth like jagged teeth.

"Have you heard from your mum yet?" Tom asked as they turned off State Highway 1 and headed into the Wairau Valley, towards the mountains.

"Not yet."

"Try not to worry about it," Tom said. Tom reached across and gave his leg a squeeze. "It'll be OK, you know."

He gazed out the window again, at the passing scenery. Dark clouds were rolling in from the south. It would be pouring before they reached Nelson.

They reached Motueka, on the western shore of Tasman Bay, just as it was getting dark.

Tom pulled over at the side of the road to check the map one more time. "The campsite should be just round the next corner," he said, folding up the map and tucking it away beneath the sun visor. "You hungry?"

He nodded.

"Me too, but let's get this tent up first, eh, while it's still light."

It took longer than he had thought it would take to erect a two-man tent. By the time they were hammering in the last of the pegs, it was already dark and spitting with rain.

They left their bags locked safely in the car and headed back into town in search of something to eat.

There was a fish and chip shop close to the campsite, but since it smelt of old, dirty fat, they didn't stop. Instead, they settled on a hotel on the high street. It looked as if every other person in the town had had the

212

same idea. The main bar was packed to the rafters, and they had to wait half an hour just to get a seat.

"You're not still worrying, are you?" Tom asked.

"Just a bit," he replied, looking down at his menu. "What are you having?"

Tom's phone beeped and he picked it up. A shadow passed over his face.

"Is everything OK?" he asked.

Tom put the phone down and exhaled loudly. "It's Eve."

He felt his stomach muscles clench.

He had been wondering when Tom would mention Eve. Tom hadn't mentioned her since that afternoon at his flat, when he had announced that he had broken off the relationship. Perhaps Tom felt uncomfortable broaching the subject; he knew that he certainly did.

"What does she want?" he asked. He was unable to disguise the feeling of intense jealousy that had taken over him.

Tom looked up and fixed him with a stare. "Are you OK?

"I'm fine." He took a sip of his beer and let his eyes wander round the room.

"Sam."

He looked back at Tom. "Shall we order?"

"Sam."

"What?"

"Is there something you want to talk about?"

Of course there's something I want to talk about, dick. He shook his head. "No."

They ordered their food and sat in silence until it

arrived. The television in the corner of the room was playing the highlights of the previous night's rugby test and Tom focused all his attention on the game.

He wanted to tell Tom that he was sorry, that he hadn't meant to overreact, but just as he opened his mouth, Tom turned to him and asked, "So what do you want to do tomorrow?"

The moment was gone. He shrugged his shoulder and took a bite out of his burger. Egg yolk oozed out of the sides and ran down his hands. Tom passed him a clean napkin.

"Ta," he mumbled. He finished chewing and swallowed. "I don't know. We could carry on up the coast, maybe hire some kayaks?"

Tom considered the suggestion for a moment and then nodded. "Sounds good."

Between Tom's snoring and the howling of the wind, he barely got a wink of sleep all night. He woke for the last time just before dawn, freezing cold and thoroughly miserable. Tom had rolled over onto his side of the bed, and the air mattress, unable to support the added weight, had deflated. He could feel the cold, hard earth pressing against his hipbone.

As he sat up, his head brushed against the slanted roof of the tent. The movement dislodged the moisture that had seeped through the fabric during the night and brought a cascade of droplets raining down on them.

"Fuck," Tom groaned, pulling the covers over his head, "don't touch the sides."

He ignored the outburst, rolled over onto his knees and crawled out into the fresh air. The dewy grass was

214

ice cold underfoot and by the time he made it back from the shower block, he could hardly feel his toes.

They spent the morning kayaking along the coast. The weather was stunning, the storm clouds having passed on overnight, and the surface of the ocean sparkled as it caught and reflected the sun's light. At lunch, they stopped at one of the many secluded bays, pulled the two-man canoe up onto the beach, and lay back on the sand.

"My arms hurt," he told the blue expanse above. In fact, every muscle in his body hurt. More than once, he had felt the boat go heavy and had looked over his shoulder to find Tom admiring the scenery, his paddle resting clear of the water.

Tom rolled over onto his side and propped himself up on one elbow. "So are we going to talk about last night?"

He closed his eyes and took a deep breath. "If you want to."

"I do."

A few minutes passed before Tom spoke again.

"You know there's nothing to be jealous about?"

He sat up and glared at Tom. "Who said I was jealous?"

Tom smiled and raised his eyebrows.

"Well, maybe a bit," he conceded.

"Why?" Tom laughed.

"Isn't it obvious?"

This time it was Tom who took the deep breath. "It's over between us—I mean between me and Eve. You do know that, right?"

He felt his hackles rise at the mention of her name. "Do I?"

Tom looked annoyed. Whatever Tom had been expecting him to say, that wasn't it. "What do you mean 'Do I?'?"

He didn't know what to say in response, so he kept his mouth clamped shut.

Tom got to his feet with a huff and walked down to the water's edge. For a long time, neither of them moved. Tom gazed out to sea while Sam contemplated the sand.

He was still staring at the sand when Tom turned and marched back up the beach towards him.

"Stand up," Tom said.

His heart dropped but he did as he was told. He couldn't bring himself to look Tom in the face, though.

Tom gripped his chin with one hand and forced him to make eye contact.

"There's only you," Tom said, giving his face a gentle shake. "There's only been you for three fucking years."

He swallowed and tried to look down but Tom wouldn't let him.

"Do you hear me?"

He nodded his head as best he could.

"Good."

Tom smiled and kissed him before he could respond.

The next morning, they packed up the car and hit the road while the rest of the campsite was still asleep. And since neither of them needed to be in Wellington on Monday, they took the road heading south, towards Lewis Pass, and the east coast beyond.

"Mind if we join you?"

He shuffled along the bench seat to let the two girls sit

down. It was freezing cold outside, and it looked as if the entire population of Kaikoura was trying to squeeze into the pub on the Esplanade.

"Here you go," Tom said, handing him a pint of beer.

It looks more like stout, he thought.

"It's a local brew. The barman recommended it." Tom took a sip and tilted his head slightly. "Actually, it's not bad."

He noticed that the two girls had stopped talking and were now watching Tom intently. Before he had a chance to taste the beer for himself, the girl sitting next to him leaned across the table. "I'm Sarah," she said, offering Tom a hand, "and this is Kate."

Tom put down his drink. He introduced himself and then nodded across the table. "And that's Sam."

Sarah gave him a perfunctory glance and then turned her attention back to Tom. "So are you staying in Kaikoura long?" she asked. She swayed in her seat as she spoke. Clearly, the drink she was holding wasn't her first—or second.

"No, we're just passing through on our way home," Tom replied, with a polite smile.

"We're up from Christchurch for a few days," Sarah continued. She sucked coquettishly on the straw in her glass. She was flirting so obviously that it was almost amusing. "So isn't your girlfriend with you, then?"

Tom smiled again, but Sam saw his Adam's apple twitch.

"I don't have a girlfriend," Tom replied.

He could hear the wariness in Tom's voice, but clearly Sarah didn't. "So you're not seeing anyone at the moment then?" she continued to probe.

Tom hunched his shoulders as if the shirt that he was wearing had suddenly shrunk several sizes. "No."

His voice was barely audible, but still it rang in Sam's ears.

Tom glanced in his direction and then looked away.

In hindsight, he shouldn't have been as bothered as he was. What had he been expecting? That Tom bare his soul to a complete stranger?

Still, Tom's answer cut him to the quick. *You obviously don't mean as much to him as you thought*, a voice in his head whispered.

He put down his drink and got to his feet. "I'm heading off," he announced.

"Wait—I'll come with you," Tom said, pushing back his chair to stand up, but Sam cut him off.

"No, stay." He turned and walked away before Tom had a chance to object.

A full hour passed before Tom unzipped the front of the tent and climbed in beside him. The inflatable mattress ballooned under the added weight and he rolled against the side.

"I'm sorry." Tom's voice broke the silence that hung heavy between them. It was pitch-black and he couldn't see Tom's face, but he knew he was close; heat emanated from his body like a radiator.

"No, I'm sorry," he replied with a sigh.

He could almost feel the tension dissolve.

He waited for Tom to speak, but he didn't, and they lay in silence again.

"Do you suppose it'll gets easier?" Tom asked at last, just when he was beginning to think that Tom had fallen asleep.

218

He took a moment to reply. "I really don't know."

Tom seemed to weigh up the answer before continuing. "Are you still annoyed?"

He suddenly felt incredibly foolish. "No," he lied. He rolled towards Tom and tentatively reached out a hand. His eyes had adjusted to the darkness but still he could see only the faint outline of Tom's body.

As soon as Tom felt his touch, he clasped his hand to his chest.

"Sam," Tom said, rolling over to face him and resting his forehead against his own. He could feel the warmth of Tom's breath on his face. "Can I ask you something?"

His whole body tensed. "OK," he replied warily.

Mentally, he was bracing himself for the worst. So when Tom asked, "Will you go out with me?", he actually laughed.

"Hey," Tom complained but didn't let go of his hand. He continued to hold it against his heart.

"Sorry, it just wasn't what I was expecting you to say."

Hopefully it was dark enough to hide the absurd grin on his face.

"So?" Tom asked.

"Hmm," he joked, "I suppose I could."

Tom grabbed him around the waist and dug his fingers into his side, making him squeal like a stuck pig. "What did you say?"

"I—said—" he gasped between shallow breaths. But Tom continued to tickle him mercilessly.

"What was that you said?"

"OK!" he shouted when he couldn't take any more. Tom stopped straightaway.

Tom leaned over him and brushed the hair off of his damp forehead. His chest was pounding.

"That's better," Tom said. Tom was close enough now that he could see the smile on his face.

Tom leaned down and kissed him and the world around them disappeared.

chapter fourteen

HE HAD HIS hands in a sink full of hot, soapy water when he heard footsteps on the linoleum floor behind him.

"Argh, you're all wet," he squirmed as Tom nuzzled the back of his neck. Tom had only just showered and his hair was still dripping wet. A trickle of cold water ran down Sam's spine and made him shiver. He turned and wiped his hands on the towel around Tom's waist.

"Hi," Tom grinned, pushing him back against the benchtop and planting a kiss on his lips. He could feel a hardness against his stomach, and when he reached beneath the towel, Tom's whole body shuddered in response.

Tom bit his earlobe teasingly and then led him through the empty flat, to the bedroom.

"I thought we could go to the golf club tonight," Tom said when they were lying in bed some time later.

His head was resting on Tom's chest, and he could hear Tom's heart beating just centimetres below. His own heart was still pounding.

He took a deep breath. "I don't know," he said, running his fingers lightly over Tom's flat stomach and playing with the fair hair just below his bellybutton.

Several weeks had passed since the showdown at his parents' house, but the memory of it all was still uncomfortably fresh. "You don't think it might be too soon?"

Tom had been stroking his hair. Tom stopped and pushed himself up on his elbows, forcing him to sit up as well.

"We can't hide away for ever," Tom protested. "And, anyway, we've got just as much right to be there as anybody. I pay my subs too."

"But what if my dad is there?"

He was quickly learning that Tom had a stubborn streak of his own. "Let's just go for one drink, eh?" Tom persisted.

"OK," he agreed reluctantly.

It was every bit as horrendous as he had been expecting. When they walked through the door, all conversation stopped and an awkward silence descended on the club.

As well as his father, whose face blanched the moment he saw them, Jarryd was there too. He was standing at the bar, talking to Ngaire. He put down his drink and walked straight over.

"How's it going, bro?" Tom said, holding out a hand to his best friend.

He knew that Tom hadn't spoken to Jarryd since he had broken things off with Eve.

He held his breath.

There was a moment of silence and then Jarryd swiped his palm against Tom's and pulled Tom towards him with his fingertips. "Good to see you, bro," he said, slapping Tom on the back hard.

He exhaled. Only then did he realise just how tense he had actually been.

"And you too, Sam," Jarryd said, turning and offering him a hand. "What has it been? Two or three years?"

"Something like that," he replied.

Jarryd filled two clean glasses from the jug in the centre of the table and handed one to each of them. "Cheers."

He didn't pay much attention to the conversation. All he could think about what his father, standing in the corner behind him. He could almost feel his father's eyes burning two holes in his back.

It was the look of alarm on Tom's face that came as the first warning. He didn't need to look to know that his father was standing right behind him.

Slowly he turned around. "Dad."

"What do you think you're doing?" his father cut to the chase.

Tom stepped up beside him. "We don't want any trouble, John. We're just here for a quiet drink."

His father didn't even look at Tom; he kept his gaze fixed on him. "It's got absolutely nothing to do with you," he hissed through clenched teeth.

A couple of his father's buddies had gathered behind him. For a moment, he was reminded of Sutcliffe and his two sidekicks. He almost laughed.

"This is ridiculous, Dad," he said. "I don't want to fight with you."

His father's eyes flared, but before the situation had a chance to escalate, Ngaire strode into the mix.

"Go home to your wife, John," she said, standing

between them, her arms crossed. She was an indomitable force even when she wasn't annoyed, and his father backed away instinctively. "The boy's done nothin' wrong, and I won't have you causing a scene."

His father's friends dropped away one by one and returned to their drinks, leaving him standing alone.

"What's his problem?" Jarryd said, after his father had stormed out the bar. It was more of a statement than a question.

Ngaire smiled and patted him on the shoulder. Then she went back to emptying the ashtrays into a bucket with an old paintbrush.

The television behind the bar was tuned to Sky Sports. Within minutes Jarryd and Tom were engrossed in the Friday night football.

"So what you gonna do for work now then, eh?" Jarryd asked the next time the whistle blew. He kept his eyes on the screen, though, and before Tom could answer, he was shouting at the live-action replay. "Are you fucking blind, ref? Knock on. Jeez!"

Jarryd tutted and shook his head as the word TRY flashed up on the screen in large green letters.

"I've been thinking about that a lot actually," Tom said once he had Jarryd's full attention.

Sam didn't know why he was so surprised to hear that Tom had been making plans. It was logical. The fact that most of Tom's work came from his father meant that life had the potential to get difficult, and quickly.

Jarryd turned and raised his eyebrows. "Go on."

"I'm done with earning peanuts working for the man. I've got my ticket now, so what's stopping me from

224

going out on my own? Hell, you should join me."

Jarryd contemplated the suggestion for a moment. "OK," he nodded, "but you'll have to do the books. I'm not too flash with numbers."

The smile that lit up Tom's face made the past hour worthwhile.

HE NOTICED EVE before Tom did. She was sitting on the footpath outside his flat, her head in her hands. Even at a distance, it was obvious that she had been drinking heavily. When she saw them both, she staggered to her feet and stumbled forward.

"Wait here," Tom said, motioning to him to stand well back. And for once, he was more than happy to do as he was told.

Sam was too far away to be able to hear everything that Tom was saying, but the words "sorry", "home" and "over" rang out crystal clear. Unfortunately, those weren't the words that Eve had wanted to hear.

Her face hardened and she struck out like a wild animal. Tom managed to deflect the blow in time. Had she been sober, though, her fist would almost certainly have connected with his nose. Tom held her against him in a bear hug.

"Let go of me, you bastard," she hissed, struggling to free her arms for another strike.

Thank God nobody is around to witness this, Sam thought, glancing behind him. Two guys restraining a girl in a dark street didn't look good.

Eve managed to wrestle herself free at last. She staggered backwards, panting.

"What are you staring at?" she screamed, lunging towards him, but Tom managed to catch her again. "He'll only hurt you," she yelled, her voice softening as if she were giving advice to a friend.

She turned her head and spat at Tom. Tom let go immediately.

He wanted to run to Tom, to protect him, but he hung back out of fear of making things worse.

Thankfully, Eve seemed to have grown tired of fighting. She crumpled like a marionette whose strings had gone slack.

Tom stepped towards her and tentatively placed a hand on her shoulder. This time, instead of batting his hand away, she clasped it in hers and started to sob.

It was past midnight by the time Tom got back to the flat. He flopped down onto the bed and closed his eyes. He looked exhausted.

"Did you get her home OK?" Sam asked, but Tom just groaned in reply. "That bad, eh?"

Tom rolled over onto his front and rested his head in Sam's lap. "I feel like the biggest shit in the world."

He stroked Tom's hair. "No, that title belongs to my dad, surely?"

Tom gave a half-hearted laugh. "True. But I'd come a close second, according to Eve."

chapter fifteen

Tom reached for the first blunt object he could find and crept along the hall. He remembered closing off the living room before going to bed—he always did, to keep out the cat, who was systematically destroying the furniture—but the door was now ajar.

He held the unopened bottle of wine by its neck and raised it above his head.

"Hello," he called out. He had hoped the cat would come skulking through the gap, but he didn't. "Is there anybody there?"

Adrenalin was coursing through his veins, in anticipation of a fight. He gripped the bottle tighter, ready to swing if needed.

The silence was broken by a loud, mucus-filled sniff. A human sniff.

An intruder with a nasty cold? He flung open the door and flicked on the light.

"Olivia," he exhaled with relief and lowered the bottle to his side. "What the hell?"

His niece was sitting on the sofa. As soon as she saw him, her face crumpled.

"I didn't…know…where…to go," she tried to explain between sobs.

He sat down next to her and put an arm around her shoulder. Her body was like one giant ice cube. What had she been doing? Wandering around in the cold all night? He felt her relax as she nestled into him.

"I'm sorry," she mumbled into his chest.

"Ssh," he replied, rubbing some warmth into her frozen body. He had never seen his niece so upset before—not even when Sam had died. Then she had withdrawn into herself, like a pipi retreating into its shell.

He put his hand in his pocket and produced a scrunched up tissue. He offered it to her.

"Thanks." She wiped her nose and sat up straight.

He looked her in the eyes. "You're not pregnant, are you?"

When she shook her head, he exhaled with relief. "Thank Christ for that."

He stood up and walked over to the French doors, which opened out onto the deck. A possum was ferreting around on the lawn below. As soon as it saw movement inside the house, it shot up the nearest tree.

"What, then? You're not sick, are you?" he asked turning back to face her. A pit had formed in his stomach. Olivia shook her head, but the nausea remained. "Your mother, then. She's OK, isn't she?" The possibilities were coming thick and fast now.

"He's been cheating on me," Olivia answered, her voice almost a whisper.

"Who—" he began to say, but then he remembered the boy she had mentioned in the car on their way to Castlepoint. "Oh."

228

He walked across the room and stood silently at her side. *If only Sam were here,* he thought. He would have known what to say.

He leaned forward and plucked a clean tissue from the box on the coffee table. "Here, blow your nose properly." He gave her shoulder a squeeze. "I'll make us some tea."

"You haven't got anything stronger, have you?"

He almost laughed but managed to check the impulse in time. She was no longer a child—he could see that now—but a young woman who was hurting immensely.

She followed him into the kitchen and slumped onto a chair. He kept an eye on her reflection in the window as he poured out two glasses of red wine. "Here," he said, handing her a glass. He had only half filled it. "Don't tell your mother, though."

A faint smile flashed across her face and was then gone.

She took a sip and reached across the table, to one of the many piles of photographs that he had arranged in date order.

"Where was this taken?" She held up a photo of him, sunbathing on a white, sandy beach. The ocean in the background was turquoise.

"Rarotonga," he replied. He took a sip from his own glass.

"And this one?" she continued, reaching for another pile at random. She held up a photo of Sam in front of a temple. A monkey was perched on his shoulder.

"Cambodia."

"I don't remember you guys going there?"

"You were just a kid at the time."

"And this one?" She pointed to a photo of him, holding a fish that was the size of a small dog.

"The Bay of Islands."

He put down his glass of wine and leaned back in his seat. "You didn't come here to look at old photos. Now tell me what happened."

The sadness returned to her face at once and he felt ashamed of himself for not letting her continue on the trip down memory lane.

"George dumped me," she replied. She seemed visibly to deflate before his eyes.

"Go on?" he prompted. He could see there was more that she wanted to say, but he kept quiet, allowing her to take the time she needed.

"I really loved him," she said at last. A solitary tear broke free and ran down her cheek. He reached across the table and placed a hand over hers. "I suppose you're going tell me I'm too young to know what love is?" she continued. There was an accusatory tone to her voice. He could almost feel the anger thrumming through her body.

"I would never tell you that," he said, still holding her hand. Her shoulders slumped and she turned her attention back to the photographs.

"Tell me about Sam."

He let go of her hand and took a deep breath. "What do you want to know?"

"How long were you together?"

"Eleven years." He could see her trying to do the maths inside her head. "You were five when we met. Don't you remember?"

She tilted her head to the side, thinking. "Perhaps. I'm not really sure, to be honest. It seems like Sam was always there."

He smiled. He knew exactly what she meant.

"What did Mum say when you told her—you know?"

He didn't answer straightaway. He got to his feet and walked over to the window. The moon was full and the surrounding hills looked as if they were plated with silver. Everything looked so peaceful. "What did Carla say when she found out I was gay, you mean?"

Olivia nodded.

"She was great."

"And your friends?"

"Great too. It was never an issue, which is more than can be said for Sam's family." He was unable to disguise the bitterness he felt whenever he thought about Sam's parents. He wasn't sure how much Olivia knew about Sam's childhood—how much Carla had told her—but to his relief, she seemed happy with the information he had already provided and didn't probe any deeper.

"When do you leave?" she asked, changing the subject completely.

"A week on Tuesday. I fly to Auckland first, and then direct to Santiago."

"And after that?"

He shrugged his shoulders, "Who knows? I have an open ticket, so I'll just go wherever the wind blows me, I suppose."

Olivia looked away before she spoke again. "I'm going to miss you while you're gone."

He smiled. He would miss his niece more than she

would ever know. He cleared his throat. "I know I don't say this often, but thank you. I appreciate your support this past year."

He got to his feet and placed the empty wine glasses in the sink. Then he picked up the phone and handed it to Olivia.

"Here, phone your mum and tell her where you are so that she doesn't worry. I'll make up the spare bed."

chapter sixteen

"WILL YOU PLEASE just go and see the doctor?"

Sam lifted his head out of the bucket and glared at Tom. He knew Tom was right—he hadn't felt well for weeks now; months if he thought about it objectively—but he had been hoping the nausea would go away of its own accord. Going to the doctor's never ended well. Once they started poking and prodding, they almost always found something wrong.

"I will," he groaned and dry retched again.

"I'll make you an appointment now." Tom picked up the phone and wandered out of the room. If he had had even slightly more energy, he would have followed him, stopped him, but instead, he stayed put, the bucket gripped between his knees.

"He can see you this afternoon," Tom said, appearing in the doorway a few minutes later. "I'll come home early from work and take you."

Tom turned to leave and then stopped. "Perhaps I should call in sick today."

"No," he said as authoritatively as he could manage.

Tom opened his mouth to protest but then closed it

again. Silently, he helped him back into bed, plumped up the pillows behind his back and placed the television remote within easy reach.

"I'll be fine," he said, feeling guilty for worrying Tom, "I've probably just got some gastro bug. There's been something doing the rounds at work lately."

"I can probably stay for a bit—" Tom stopped when he saw the look on his face.

"Just go, will you," he said. He tried to smile as he reached for one of the decorative cushions and threw it at Tom. It fell several feet short.

Tom returned his smile, but the concern didn't leave his eyes.

Once he was sure that Tom wouldn't return, he threw back the covers and hauled himself to the edge of the bed. Just getting to his feet seemed to zap all his energy at the moment. He had to stand still and wait for the fog in his head to clear before he could continue.

The light in the bathroom was poor, but it was still obvious that something wasn't quite right. The whites of his eyes still had a yellow tinge to them. And his face, usually a healthy olive colour, was looking more and more pale and drawn.

He ran his fingers over his cheeks. He could feel the outline of the bones underneath. He had lost weight, too.

By the time Tom returned home to take him to his appointment, he was dressed and sitting on the sofa.

"Have you eaten anything?" Tom asked before saying hello.

He shook his head. "I haven't been hungry."

"Get your coat then, or we'll miss the appointment."

234

He opened his mouth to say something smart but felt another wave of nausea bubble up from the pit of his stomach and had to close his eyes and hold the back of his hand against his lips.

"How long have you been feeling this way?" the doctor asked.

"A few weeks," he replied.

"Do you think it could be concussion still?" Tom interrupted. "He took a golf ball to the head recently."

The doctor pushed his glasses up on to the bridge of his nose and tapped something into his computer. "Let's see, shall we?"

He gave Tom a frustrated glare, but Tom continued, "Every day it's the same. We thought it might be food poisoning at first, and then, when it continued past a few days, we assumed it was one of those gastro bugs."

"I see," the doctor said.

He gasped as the stethoscope touched his bare back. "Take a deep breath." He did as he was told and the doctor moved the cold metal disc to another spot. "And another."

He kept his eyes closed so that he wouldn't have to look at Tom.

The doctor finished the examination, typed some more notes into the computer, and reached into a drawer beside his desk.

"Take this," the doctor said, handing him a small plastic container. "Fill it with urine and hand it to the nurse at the pathology clinic indicated on the form. Are you able to go there now? I'd like to do some blood tests." He directed the question at Tom, who nodded.

"What kind of blood tests?" he asked hesitantly; he wasn't at all sure he wanted to know the answer. He clasped his hands between his legs to disguise their shaking. Hopefully, Tom hadn't seen.

"Try not to worry," the doctor replied. "We'll have a better idea what we're dealing with in a few days' time."

He noticed that the doctor hadn't answered his question, but he decided not to press the point. He stood and followed Tom silently out the door.

The doctor called with the results early the next day.

"Here—it's for you," Tom said, pressing his lips into a smile as he handed him the phone.

The conversation was short, and when he thought back on it later, he wasn't able to remember half of what the doctor had said.

"He wants me to go to the hospital for more tests," he told Tom, hanging up the telephone. "He's making an appointment right away."

"What type of tests?" Tom asked. The alarm in his voice was crystal clear.

He shrugged and sank down onto the nearest chair. All he could hear was his own pulse thumping in his ears. His throat was dry and he gagged as he tried to swallow.

"I think I'm going to be sick," he mumbled. Tom sprinted out of the room for the bucket and only just made it back in time.

The first appointment with the consultant didn't answer many of his questions, but by the time his second appointment rolled around, it was impossible to deny the seriousness of the situation any longer. He could barely keep his food down, and he had had to tighten his belt another notch.

"They don't tell you to come in when it's good news, do they?" he answered shortly and instantly regretted it. Tom was looking exhausted too. "Sorry," he apologised and gave Tom's hand a squeeze. Tom squeezed back but he continued to stare at the wall opposite.

He looked at his watch for the second time in as many minutes. "Why can't they ever run on time?" He tossed the out-of-date magazine that he was reading back onto the table. "They wouldn't get away with it in the real world."

"God, I wish this wasn't the real world," Tom sighed. He took a deep breath and leaned his head against the wall.

Five minutes later, the receptionist called out his name and they made their way silently to the consultant's office.

Is it the detergent they use or the smell of sickness that gives all hospitals the same smell? He let his gaze wander around the room. *Or perhaps it's the smell of fear.* He felt detached, as if he were watching from afar.

"Cancer of the what?" Tom's voice pierced the numbness and, suddenly, he was right back in the room.

"Cancer of the pancreas," the grey-haired consultant repeated. He placed his elbows on the desk and pressed his fingertips together to form a peak. "I won't lie to you. The results aren't good."

Although he had been preparing himself for the worst, the words still dealt him a sucker punch to the stomach.

"Cancer of the pancreas." He tried the words out for

size, as if he were trying to speak a language that he didn't understand.

The doctor started to explain the options that were open to him, but the words washed over his head and flowed on out the door.

"How bad?" Tom asked the only question of importance.

He didn't hear the answer but the look of sympathy on the doctor's face told him all he needed to know.

As HIS EYES adjusted to the darkness, the bedroom slowly took shape around him. First, the television came into view, its screen a silvery shade of grey; next the wardrobe, tall and imposing; and finally the squat chest of drawers beside the door. Objects that were so familiar, yet which now looked extraneous. Objects that would outlive him.

Tom was fast asleep beside him. He looked so peaceful. He hoped that he was dreaming of something nice.

Lying perfectly still, he almost felt like his old self. It was only when he moved that the pain got especially bad. "Am I really dying?" he asked the silence, but he didn't get an answer.

He took a deep breath and rolled onto his side. He had to bite down on his bottom lip to stop himself from crying out and waking Tom. *I guess I have my answer*, he thought, wiping the perspiration from his forehead with the hand towel that Tom had left by the bed.

Slowly, he pushed himself up onto one elbow and swung his legs over the edge of the bed. He might as well get up; he would only lie awake for the rest of the night. And lying in the dark, everything was infinitely more frightening. Awake, he could distract himself with the business of staying alive.

He hauled himself to his feet, steadying himself on the bedside table before venturing out into no-man's-land. When he did, it felt as if he were dragging lead weights behind him.

While he waited for the jug to boil, he peered out of the kitchen window, into the night. He had to cup his hands around his eyes and push his nose up against the glass to see through his reflection. Down on the flat, the streetlamps flickered like fireflies.

His hands shook as he poured the boiling water, and then the milk, into the cup. By the time he had mopped up the mess, he was thoroughly exhausted.

Tom had left a syringe full of morphine on the bench. He picked it up and squirted the bitter liquid into the back of his mouth. Most of the time the morphine driver attached to his arm kept the pain at bay, but every so often he needed a top-up.

An hour or so passed before he heard any movement downstairs. He was sitting in silence, the television on mute, reading the subtitles when Tom appeared in the doorway.

"Another bad dream?" Tom asked, stifling a yawn.

"No, I just couldn't sleep," he replied truthfully this time. "Go back to bed. I'm fine, really."

Watching Tom run himself into the ground only added to the pain. He sincerely hoped that Tom would find some peace when he was gone.

Tom ignored him and sat down on the sofa. He felt the cushions dip under the added weight.

"Please call her," Tom said. "I know you say you don't want to, but I don't believe you. I know you."

He felt his shoulders tense but he managed to keep his annoyance in check. "You know me?" he smiled wryly.

"Yes, Sam Wilson. I know you." Tom looked him in the eye and held his gaze.

"Maybe you're right," he conceded at last and looked away. "But I can't call her now. Have you seen what time it is?"

Tom laughed and clapped him on the knee. The movement sent a jarring pain up his leg.

They sat together, cuddled up beneath a blanket, until it was daylight outside. Usually he had to keep a hot-water bottle by him at all times, but Tom's body was giving off enough heat for the both of them. He rested his head against Tom's shoulder, enjoying the warmth.

"Shall I call her for you?" Tom said.

He didn't respond straight away. "No, I'll do it. I wouldn't inflict that on you." He felt rather than heard Tom chuckle.

"Don't go—not just yet," he said, clutching at Tom's arm to stop him from getting up. Tom sank back onto the sofa and pulled him close. He rested his head on Tom's chest.

A tear ran down his cheek, onto Tom's T-shirt. Then another, and another. It wouldn't be long before Tom felt the damp patch against his skin. "I'm sorry," he mumbled.

"What for?" Tom asked. He felt Tom's lips against his bald scalp.

"For dying."

Tom's body stiffened but his embrace got tighter. His bones seemed to be grinding against each other but he would have endured any amount of pain to stay the way there were for a few moments longer.

"I called her," Tom said, walking back into the room carrying a plate of toast. Tom offered him a slice but he shook his head.

"I can't—I'm sorry." He turned his head away. Even the smell of food made him want to vomit. "So what did she say?"

Tom put the plate down on the sideboard, well away from where he was sitting. "She's coming over this morning. I told her not to come before ten, though."

It was barely nine o'clock when the doorbell rang. Tom had only just disappeared downstairs for a shower. He levered himself off the sofa and made his way to the front door, holding on to the furniture for support. The doorbell rang a second time before he had even reached the hall.

"I'm coming," he croaked, covering the last couple of metres with one, Herculean effort and grabbing hold of the door handle. He leaned all his weight against the frame and took several deep breaths. When his head had stopped spinning, he put his shoulders back and open the door. "Hi, Mum."

His mother raised her head and her face assumed a look of absolute horror. "Oh, Sam," she gasped, bringing her hands together in front of her mouth as if in prayer. "Oh, Sam, my poor boy."

"Why don't you come in?" he said, ignoring the outburst.

He hadn't heard Tom approach, but when he turned, Tom was standing right behind him. Instinctively, he reached back and held on to Tom's arm. His mother bristled.

"Hello," Tom said, but she walked straight past him as if he didn't exist.

It was a year since he had seen his mother, and she seemed to have aged at least ten years in that time. Her hair, now completely white, was pulled back over her scalp and tied neatly in a bun.

She looks so old, so fragile, he thought, watching in silence as she wandered around the unfamiliar room, her handbag clutched to her chest like a lifesaver. Many times he had imagined showing his mother his home for the first time. Never had he envisaged that it would be under such circumstances.

Instinctively, he wanted to reach out to her, to comfort her, but something held him back. His mother seemed to sense his indecision and looked up. He turned away. The memory of their last argument was still too raw. "Just go," she had told him—his own mother. "You're not welcome here any more."

"What do you want, Mum?" he said. He watched as she squared her shoulders and raised her chin in a gesture of defiance. "Tell me the truth, Sam," she said. "Is it AIDS?"

He didn't think his mother could shock him any more, but apparently he was wrong. He stared at her in disbelief. "Would it matter if it was?" he asked.

"I know you hate me," she said, ignoring the question completely.

He sighed and sat down on the nearest chair. He

couldn't stand a moment longer.

"No, I don't hate you," he replied. He felt worn out already and she had been in the house less than five minutes. "Why are you here, Mum?" he asked again.

She paused for a moment before replying. "It's been so hard since your dad died. I know we didn't have the perfect marriage—"

He scoffed. He couldn't help himself. "He beat you black and blue, for heaven's sake, Mum."

"He had his faults, but I loved him. And he loved me," she said, as if defying him to contradict her.

"Would you like a cup of tea?" Tom interrupted. His mother accepted with a solitary nod and Tom escaped to the kitchen.

"Sam, won't you please let Father Maguire visit you?" his mother said as soon as Tom was out of earshot.

"What for?" he asked.

"Sam, it's not too late to repent." His mother kept glancing at the door as if she expected the Devil to appear at any moment. "God will forgive. The Bible promises us—"

He had heard enough; she hadn't changed and never would. "Stop," he said. "I want you to leave now."

His mother leaned forward and clutched at his hands but he pulled them away.

She stood and walked past Tom, who had just appeared with a tray of tea and biscuits. When she reached the door, she stopped and turned. "Your father repented and he is now at peace. I hope I will be able to say the same for you."

For three days and three nights, Tom stayed by Sam's bedside, wandering only as far as the vending machine at the end of the hall when his hunger got the better of him. His sister had begged him to go home and rest, promising to stay with Sam in his place, but he had ignored her. Sleep could wait.

Sam's skeletal body was almost hidden beneath the blankets, and the room, which was bathed in a perpetual twilight by the blinds, was beginning to smell.

"You should get some sleep," his sister said, reaching across the bed and squeezing his hand. He shook his head and ran his fingers through his hair.

"I've got to go," she continued. "But I'll be back first thing in the morning. Call me if anything changes, and I'll come straight away." He nodded.

A never-ending stream of visitors had been filing in and out of the room all day, and he was glad finally to have some peace.

Sam groaned and opened his eyes.

"I'm here," he said gently, sitting up with a start and slipping his hand into Sam's. He felt Sam's fingers clench ever so slightly. "You've been asleep."

He watched as Sam's eyes scanned the room. He seemed to be looking for a point of reference. His eyes were only half open and the whites were now completely yellow.

"I'm here," he repeated, moving into Sam's line of vision. He saw the muscles in Sam's face relax instantly.

"You've been snoring." He smiled, dipping a fresh cotton swab into the glass of lukewarm water next to the bed and carefully wetting Sam's lips. They soaked

244

up the water like a dry riverbed, and Sam let out a groan of thanks.

"That better?" he asked. Sam nodded his head just a fraction.

"Lots of people have been to see you today. Neil came by with his new girlfriend. She seems nice. I think this one might actually have gotten under his skin. It'll be interesting to see how that pans out. I hope for his sake it lasts, because I don't think he's ever had his heart broken before. Still, it might be good for him to be on the receiving end for once. And your sister visited. She didn't stay long. She had to get back to feed the kids."

Banalities flowed from his mouth. What he really wanted to say was buried too deep for him to get to right now.

He sat back down and pulled the chair up as close to the bed as possible. Gently, so as not to cause any movement, he rested his head on the pillow next to Sam's. Their noses were almost touching and each time Sam exhaled he had to fight back the urge to gag.

"Love you," he whispered, just loud enough for Sam to hear. Sam sighed and closed his eyes. Within minutes he was asleep again.

This is not how death is supposed to happen, he thought, leaning back in his chair and stretching out his legs. *It never ends like this in the movies—the dying always look impeccable.*

Sam was still breathing, albeit more softly, when he woke an hour or two later. He jumped to his feet and stared down at Sam's wasted body. It was in exactly the same position as before, and only once he had seen Sam's chest inflate and deflate half a dozen times did he sit back down.

When Sam started to make a gurgling, choking sound an hour or two later, he flew out of the room in a blind panic.

"Try not to be alarmed." The ward matron put an arm around his shoulder and ushered him into the family room. She closed the door behind them. She remained perfectly composed in her spotless cotton uniform. "What you can hear is just the sound of air passing over the fluid that has collected in the back of his throat. He's not in any distress, I can assure you."

He didn't feel reassured in the slightest.

He returned to Sam's room and sank back into the recliner with a groan. Every muscle in his body ached with tiredness and his head was throbbing as if he had gone ten rounds in the ring.

I'll just rest my eyes for a few minutes, he told himself, leaning his head against the back of the chair. The next thing he knew, it was light outside, and an eerie silence had descended on the room.

Still half asleep, he lifted his head and rubbed the sleep from his eyes.

As soon as he looked at Sam, he knew it was all over. His chest was perfectly still and the rasping sound in his throat had stopped.

Slowly, he reached over and touched Sam's left hand, which was lying on top of the covers. The skin was cold and lifeless, like a slab of meat. He recoiled.

Unsure what he was supposed to do next, he sat and stared at Sam's lifeless body. He had never seen a dead person before. When his father died, he had gone out in the morning and simply never come home. His mother had refused to take him to the morgue; she had said it would be too traumatising. It wasn't something children should see. It would seem that she was right.

Sam's mouth was open and he reached over to close it. "You're catching flies," he said, as if everything were perfectly normal. But when he tried to push Sam's jaw closed, it wouldn't move. He tried one more time and stopped.

When the doctors arrived to certify the death, he allowed himself to be shepherded back to the family room by the kindly nurse, who made him a cup of hot tea with plenty of sugar. He took one sip and put it down. The sweetness was nausea inducing.

He returned to the room to find all the lines and tubes had been removed from Sam's body. Stripped of all the paraphernalia, his body looked even more fragile than Tom could ever have imagined. He stared in disbelief, unable to reconcile the alien he was looking at with the person he had loved.

He followed the orderlies down the corridor in a daze, his eyes glued to the metal gurney that bore Sam's body. Everything felt surreal. He wanted to peel back the covers to check that they weren't carrying away the wrong person.

The lift doors opened with a joyless ding and they all shuffled in alongside the body. There was barely enough room to move. *Sam wouldn't like this*, he thought instinctively. Sam had always hated confined spaces.

"Wait!" a voice called out just as the doors were closing.

A Filipino nurse appeared. She stuck an arm through the gap to stop the doors from closing. "It's the mother."

The sight of Sam's mother being escorted gently towards the lift, a short man with close-cropped grey hair, spectacles and a pure brilliant white dog collar in tow, was more than he could bear. He was out of the lift and striding down the corridor before he knew what he was doing. "Get her out of here," he roared at the top of his lungs.

"Please, sir," the Filipino nurse tried to explain as she chased after him, "it's the mother."

But he was past listening. He grabbed Sam's mother by the arm. He was so angry his hands were shaking. "How dare you come here playing the grieving mother," he said, squeezing her arm as he would have liked to wring her neck. "You're too late—too late."

To give Sam's mother her due, she didn't even flinch. She raised her nose and looked past him defiantly.

"Sir, I need you to let go now." A middle-aged security guard appeared at his side as if from nowhere. Reluctantly, he released his grip.

"Is something the matter, sir?" the guard asked, manoeuvring himself in front of Sam's mother.

He stared at the guard, open-mouthed. "Yes, something is the matter," he said. "Get this fucking woman out of here, or I will."

"I'm not going anywhere," Sam's mother piped up from behind the security guard's back. "He was my son and I want him to have a Christian burial. Isn't it enough that you corrupted him while he was alive?"

"How dare you turn up here with your demands?" he said, brushing the security guard aside as if he weighed no more than a small child. "You have no rights," he said.

He dragged Sam's mother along the corridor, past the swelling crowd of onlookers, and shoved her through the double doors at the end.

He didn't realise it was possible to feel so angry. Fury seethed from his every pore. "Where were you when your son needed you, eh?" He flung her arm away in disgust. She recoiled against the far wall and leaned on the handrail.

"Where were you when your son was lying on the sofa in agony? When he was puking up blood? Each time he went to the hospital for yet more chemo? When he fucking died?"

She held his gaze for a moment and then looked away.

He covered his face with his hands. Right now, all he could see was Sam's lifeless body, his features wasted beyond recognition.

"Where were you?" he repeated, almost to himself. He shook his head to dislodge the mental image, but it refused to budge.

"I'm sorry," he said, raising his hands in surrender when the security guard appeared. He was too tired to fight any more. Let them do their worst.

At best, he would be trespassed from the hospital; at worst, he could expect to see the inside of a cell at the watch house on Victoria Street.

But to his surprise, instead of reading him the riot act, the guard smiled warmly. "Let's get you back to where you belong, eh?"

He almost burst into tears right there in the foyer.

Of all the times to cry, he thought, rubbing at his eyes with his fingers.

chapter seventeen

Tom nudged the front door open with his right foot.

"Far out," he groaned, dumping the shopping bags onto the hall floor. He massaged his fingers just below the knuckles until he could feel the blood flowing through them again. The string handles had cut grooves into his skin.

A quick visit to the local tramping store had netted almost everything on his list. He wasn't sure how he was going to fit it all into his backpack, let alone carry it halfway up a mountain, but he would worry about that later; right now, he would just enjoy the rare feeling of achievement.

"Why, hello," he smiled, glancing down at Bentley, who was weaving around his ankles, his tail flicking from side to side like a metronome. "You hungry, puss?"

Bentley meowed as if in response, then padded over to one of the large paper bags, sniffed at it cautiously, and rubbed the side of his mouth against one of its corners.

Reluctantly, Tom turned his attention to the growing pile of unopened mail on the sideboard. He couldn't ignore it any longer. He picked up the assortment of envelopes and flicked through the first few. *Power bill, bank statement, junk mail.*

"Damn them," he cursed, ripping open the next envelope, which was addressed to Sam. He had notified every organisation he could think of, but still the letters kept coming. How many more people would he have to tell all his business to?

With a sigh, he returned the envelopes to the sideboard—he would deal with them later—gathered up the shopping bags, and carried them the short distance to the kitchen.

He had called past the bottle shop on his way home from the tramping store. The wine bottles clinked as he set the bags down on the kitchen bench.

Bentley was already waiting by the pantry. He meowed and pawed at the door.

He had just finished unpacking when Jarryd arrived.

"I said to come around for a quiet drink," he said, helping Jarryd with the twelve-packs of beer that he was carrying under each arm.

"Stop being a big girl's blouse," Jarryd replied. He tore open one of the boxes and removed two bottles. He handed one to Tom. "You didn't think we were going to let you sneak off now, did you?"

Tom smiled. He should have known better.

"Cheers," Jarryd said, chinking bottles with him.

The beer bubbled out of the top and he had to catch it with his mouth. "It's not like I'm going for ever," he said, wiping his lips with the back of his hand. "I'll be away a few months at most."

Jarryd gave him a sceptical look and swigged his

beer. "Fuck, that's good," he said, smacking his lips and admiring the bottle, which was dripping with condensation. "So you all set then?"

As he opened his mouth to reply, the front door flew open and the other lads piled in.

Bentley was preening himself quietly in the hall. He shot into the air as if he had been electrocuted, scrambled for traction on the wooden floor, and flew out the door, down the path, and over the fence.

"Tom!" Mikey shouted. Clearly, the others had started drinking without them. Mikey clapped him on the back and dropped down onto the sofa. "Good—we haven't missed kick-off," he said, turning up the volume on the television and propping his feet on the coffee table.

"What's all this about you going overseas, eh?" Tommo asked, walking into the room, carrying several boxes of pizza. He pushed Mikey's feet off the table and set the boxes down in their place.

"I see the old bongo drums have been beating again." Tom pretended to be annoyed. In reality, he was touched that his friends cared.

"That's no way to talk about your sister," Mikey fired back at him, grinning.

He laughed, and instantly felt guilty. His eyes went to the photo of Sam on the mantelpiece. *Sorry.*

"Did I miss kick-off?" Deano asked, walking through the door a minute later and sitting down next to Mikey. He took the slice of pizza out of Mikey's hand and took a bite.

"Hey, piss off," Mikey said, snatching the slice back.

"Nah, you're all good, bro," Jarryd replied. "They're still singing. Beer?"

"Chur."

"So, South America, eh?" Tommo asked once both verses of the New Zealand anthem were over.

Mikey muted the sound for the duration of 'Advance, Australia Fair'.

"Yeah, I'm starting in Peru," he said. "And then I'll just see how I go from there."

"Peru?"

"We were always planning to go," he said, glancing at the photo again.

Tommo didn't probe any further, and they all turned their attention to the game.

The referee blew his whistle, and the Australians, having won the toss, kicked the ball straight down the field and into touch.

It wasn't long until Jarryd was yelling obscenities at the screen. "Open your fucking eyes, ref!" he cried as the Kiwi loose-head prop took a right hook to the temple during a scrum at the twenty-two-metre line. He thumped his own fist on the arm of the sofa and shook his head in disgust. By half-time, the Aussies were ten points up and he looked as if he was about to commit murder.

"I was sorry to hear about Sam, bro," Chris said during the next stoppage.

There was a collective intake of breath. Out of the corner of his eye, he saw Jarryd glare at Chris. Evidently, Jarryd had given them all strict instructions not to upset him—instructions that Chris had just flouted.

"Thanks, mate," he said, "I appreciate that."

For many of his friends, this was the first time they had

seen him since the funeral and he had been expecting the conversation to turn to Sam at some point. Chris's sigh of relief almost made him laugh.

Nate was the next to speak. "Yeah, he was a good cunt." Nate raised his bottle of beer in a toast. "To Sam."

"To Sam," they all echoed, Jarryd included.

"So how's it been—" Tommo started to ask, but Jarryd cut him off before he could finish the question. "That's enough, eh, lads? Give the boy a break."

Their questions were more endearing than distressing, yet for some reason he felt his eyes suddenly fill with tears.

Shit, shit, shit.

He jumped to his feet.

"Just going for a piss," he said, keeping his head down as he left the room.

Most of the time, he managed to keep his emotions in check, but every now and then, and always when he was least expecting it, something trivial would set him off.

"Now look what you've done," he heard Jarryd scold the others as he closed the bathroom door quietly. A tear broke free and rolled down his cheek. He brushed it away with the back of his hand.

He stood at the bathroom sink and pressed a cold flannel to his face.

When he had told his friends about Sam all those years ago, he had been expecting them to react badly. But they hadn't. They had been more accepting than he could ever have imagined. He felt ashamed for ever doubting them.

He rinsed the flannel in cold water and returned it to his eyes.

When he walked back into the room, nobody said a word. The second half of the test against Australia was well under way, and all eyes were glued to the screen.

It was at least a quarter of an hour before anybody spoke.

"So, how long are you going for?" Nate asked at last. He didn't take his eyes off the game, though.

"Not sure. Two months—perhaps three. I've got an open ticket."

"Fuck, that's mental." Mikey glanced at him and then back at the television. "The furthest I've ever been is the Gold Coast."

"What's stopping you from taking off for a few months?" he countered. "There's a whole world out there."

Mikey started to say, "It's all right for you—" and stopped. His face turned crimson. "Sorry, bro. I didn't mean to—I mean, my girlfriend might have something to say about it."

"Take her with you," he persisted, raising his eyebrows. "What's stopping you?"

Mikey pondered the question for a moment and then shrugged his shoulders. "Nothing, I suppose."

Tom skulled the last of his beer and then reached for a fresh one.

"If there's one thing I've learnt this year," he continued, removing the metal cap from the bottle. He had everybody's attention now, game or no game. "It's that life's too fucking short to put things off."

He took a sip of beer and sat back in his seat. "That's why I'm going. Now, are we watching this game or not?"

THE NEXT MORNING, he was up and out, pounding the footpaths of the eastern suburbs, while the sun was still racing westward across the South Pacific. He reached Lyall Bay at first light.

He felt surprisingly good, as if he were rediscovering a small part of himself, one he had forgotten even existed. He kicked off his running shoes and walked down to the water's edge. There wasn't a soul on the beach and he offered up a prayer of thanks to the gods.

The sand was cold and damp under foot, and he left a trail of deep prints behind him. He gasped and clenched his fists as the first wave surged around his feet, splashing ice-cold water up his calves. High above, a seagull squawked.

He walked the full length of the beach, past the surf club, rejoining the road by the rocks at the end of the bay. He brushed the sand from between his toes, slipped back into his runners and jogged on, up Onepu Road, towards Kilbirnie.

The rugby club was locked up at this hour, its windows black and uninviting, but in his head, he could hear the roar of the crowd. For a split second, he was twenty-one again, lining up to take the penalty kick that would take his team into the final.

With the roar of the crowd still ringing in his memory, he jogged on.

The kitchen window of Sam's parents' house was lit up like a goldfish bowl. He stopped on the other side of the street and stepped back into the shadows, out of sight.

A few days after Sam's showdown with his father,

Tom had gone around to the house to speak to Sam's parents, to try to sort things out once and for all.

He never told Sam. It had been an unmitigated disaster right from the start.

Sam's father had turned wild with rage, his eyes bulging from their sockets as if he were being squeezed around the middle. Tom had known he had a temper— he had worked with him often enough—but he had never experienced such anger before, and it left him speechless.

"If you don't get off my property, I'll kill you," Sam's father had shouted loud enough for the whole neighbourhood to hear. His mother hadn't said a word throughout.

Sam's father had died of stomach cancer the following year. They heard later, through Sam's sister, that his father had spent his last days in hospital, mewling like a baby.

He shook his head, remembering the stoicism that Sam had shown right up to the end.

When Sam's mother appeared at the kitchen window, he almost jumped. He stood and watched as she filled the electric jug with water, took a cup down from the shelf above the refrigerator, and made herself a cup of tea.

She looked so small and frail—a lonely old lady. He felt a pang of regret at the way things had been left between them. Regardless of her beliefs, she had loved Sam.

He took a deep breath and crossed the road, towards the house.

Just as he reached the front gate, she looked up and

saw him. She didn't flinch; she just stared, her eyes cold and lifeless.

He froze for a moment, unsure whether to continue. But he had made up his mind. He had to put things right. He pushed open the gate and stepped into the front yard.

He wasn't even halfway to the front door when Sam's mother reached for the cord that hung beside the window and lowered the blind.

THE REST OF the morning was taken up with last-minute preparations.

The cat safely deposited with his sister, he went next door to bargain with his elderly neighbour. In exchange for the lemons and feijoas off the trees in the front yard, she agreed to collect his mail and keep an eye on the house.

The first leg of the journey was a non-event. At just under an hour in duration, they had barely reached their cruising altitude when the seatbelt light pinged on and they began their descent over the Waikato Plains, towards Auckland.

He walked the short distance to the international terminal. There wasn't a breath of wind, and a handful of wispy white clouds hung motionless in the late afternoon sunshine. The peace was disturbed only momentarily by the roar of jet engines.

"Mind if I join you?"

He looked up and smiled, but inside he was cursing. He had chosen the table in the corner for one reason only: it had a perfect view of the television and the Ranfurly

Shield clash that was in full swing. "Sure," he lied.

The fat, bespectacled man shucked his jacket off and draped it over the back of a chair. He was holding a glass of beer in one hand and a tatty briefcase in the other.

"Didn't think we were going to get that try for a minute," he chortled, shuffling onto the bench seat beside him. "Marty's the name." He held out a clammy palm, which Tom begrudgingly accepted. "I'm off to Sydney. Where are you heading?"

He recoiled slightly as Marty gave a hacking cough.

"South America."

He returned his attention to the game, hoping it would become clear that he wasn't interested in conversation. But Marty didn't take the hint.

"South America, eh? I've always wanted to go there. The sheilas are supposed to be beautiful," Marty chortled and made a lewd gesture with his hands.

Tom smiled but kept his mouth closed. "Nice to meet you," he said, getting to his feet. "Good luck in Sydney."

Marty was dabbing at his brow with a dirty handkerchief. "You off now, then?" he asked. He looked visibly disappointed.

Tom nodded.

"Shame. Looks like a pretty good game."

Before he reached the edge of the bar, Marty had already turned around in his seat and was trying to engage the couple behind him in conversation. They looked about as happy about it as he had been.

He made straight for the departure gate. It was still more than an hour until boarding, but he had nothing else to do. He crossed his fingers that the flights to

South America weren't operating out of the same part of the terminal as those bound for Australia.

Just metres away, outside on the tarmac, loomed the ginormous plane that would carry him across an entire ocean. He thought of Sam, who hated flying and would have been biting his nails down to the quick if he had been here.

Slowly, the lounge filled with passengers, lone travellers like himself, as well as couples and families. Opposite, a young mother was wrestling with her infant child. He watched as she sat the boy down on the seat beside her and placed a slice of apple in his hand, but the moment her back was turned, he was off again, the apple thrown onto the floor. She abandoned her belongings to chase after him.

"Perhaps they think they'll get there before us," said the older guy sitting beside him. He nodded at the large crowd that was milling around the gate.

"Or maybe they're frightened somebody will steal their seats," his wife, or girlfriend, chuckled.

He smiled politely and went back to reading his newspaper. There was a story on the back page that he had been wanting to read. Within minutes, he was interrupted again, though.

For fuck's sake, he thought, folding the paper and looking up—straight into the eyes of the most beautiful man he had ever seen.

"Good game, eh?" the handsome stranger repeated, nodding at the paper in his lap and smiling.

"Oh, yeah—sorry," he apologised, flustered. He could feel the blood rushing to his face. "Um—did you want to read this?" He offered him the newspaper, but the guy smiled and shook his head.

"No, I'm good, ta. So where are you off to?"

"South America," he answered, and then remembered that they were both about to board the same plane. "Sorry—Peru. You?"

"Chile. My brother's teaching English there."

The guy leaned across the aisle between them and held out a hand. "Sam."

He almost snatched his hand back out of shock. "Pardon?"

"Sam. The name's Sam," the guy smiled warily.

He gulped and took a deep breath. "Sorry, ignore me. I'm a bit nervous about the flight," he lied. His heart was in his throat.

Sam got to his feet and slipped the passport and boarding pass from the back pocket of his jeans. "Looks like they're calling my row," he said, glancing down at the slip of paper. "Hey, you should give me a call if you make it to Chile," he said.

Sam took an old receipt from his wallet and scribbled on the back. "Here's my cellphone number. I'll be checking it regularly."

All of a sudden, Tom felt as if every pair of eyes in the departure lounge was looking at him. Judging.

"Thanks," he replied, folding the receipt and slipping it into the inside pocket of his jacket. "I'll text you." He held out his right hand. "It was nice to meet you."

As they shook hands, Sam's mouth turned up at the corners in a rakish grin. "You too."

He stepped to one side to let a family with small children pass. An elderly couple followed hot on their heels.

"See you on the other side then," Sam said, and with a wink, slung his backpack over one shoulder and fell in with the other passengers moving towards the gate like sheep.

What the fuck's wrong with you? he cursed himself, sitting back down and closing his eyes. He took a deep breath and let it out slowly. *He was just being friendly, you old fool.* He hoped that Sam—his Sam—wasn't up there somewhere, watching him make a complete arse of himself.

He reached into his pocket. The ink was seeping through the thin receipt already, but the numbers were still legible. He stared at the paper. Why did he feel as if he were being unfaithful? With a resigned sigh, he scrunched the slip into a ball.

"Sir."

A flight attendant was walking towards him now. How long had he been standing there, gazing into space? He looked around. The gate was almost empty.

"If you could make your way to the aircraft, please, sir," she said.

"Sorry," he apologised, reaching down for the backpack at his feet. She smiled at him before moving on to round up the other stragglers.

He took a step towards the nearest rubbish bin and stopped.

"Are you OK, sir?" The attendant appeared at his side again. This time, she looked slightly concerned.

He looked at her and then down at the scrap of paper. "Um—yes, I'm fine, thanks."

Quickly, before he changed his mind—and before they

called security—he slipped the receipt back into his pocket.

"Kia ora," the attendant at the gate greeted him. He handed over his boarding pass, which she scanned into the computer. A second later the light on the gate flashed green and the barriers blocking his path swung open. "Enjoy the flight," she said, handing him back the stub.

He took a deep breath.

So this is it.

With a clear image of Sam in his mind, he stepped forward, through the gate and into the unknown.

acknowledgments

THANK YOU FOR taking the time to read my debut novel, *SAM*. I know that *SAM* is far from the perfect novel—it's my first, after all, and I still have a lot to learn—but I am proud of it, and I hope you enjoyed the story.

I first had the idea for *SAM* in 2013, and it has taken three years of hard work, juggling early morning writing with the demands of a full-time job, to get to this point.

First and foremost, I would like to thank my family, in particular my partner, Jamie; my parents, Jan and Frank; and my grandmother June for their encouragement and support.

I would also like to thank Barbara and Chris Else and Norman Bilbrough for their critiques of my early drafts. I have learned a lot about the writing process since I started writing *SAM*, and I am excited about getting started on my next story!

I would also like to pay special thanks to Kris Lockett and Lis Sowerbutts from DIY Publishing, as well as to my copy editor, Eva Chan, for casting her expert eye over the final draft.

Please visit my website, www.lukefharris.com, for more information about me and my future projects.

Best wishes,
Luke

author bio

LUKE F HARRIS is an emergent novelist, based in Wellington, New Zealand.

Born and raised in Berkshire, England, Luke emigrated to New Zealand in 2009, where he has forged a successful career as an editor.

SAM is Luke's debut novel. For more information on Luke and his future projects, visit www.lukefharris.com